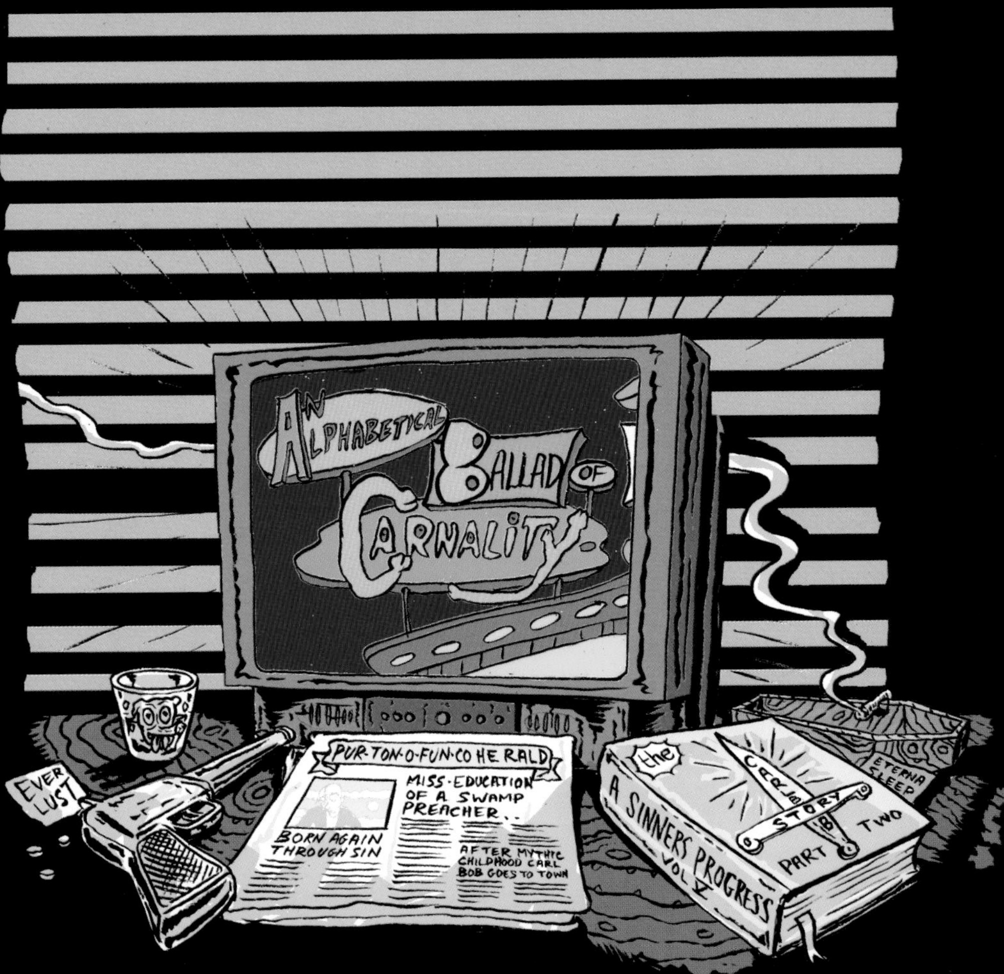
AN ALPHABETICAL BALLAD OF CARNALITY
PUR-TON-O-FUN-CO HERALD
MISS-EDUCATION OF A SWAMP PREACHER..
BORN AGAIN THROUGH SIN
AFTER MYTHIC CHILDHOOD CARL BOB GOES TO TOWN
EVER LUST
the CARL BOB STORY PART TWO
A SINNERS PROGRESS VOL V
ETERNA SLEEP

For Joni and Jake, my true loves

Story and Artwork: David Sandlin
Editor: Monte Beauchamp
Design/Art Direction/Production: Monte Beauchamp
Promotion: Eric Reynolds
Published By: Gary Groth and Kim Thompson

Fantagraphics Books, 7563 Lake City Way NE, Seattle, WA 98115
Printed in China

www.fantagraphics.com

ISBN-10: 1-56097-731-0
ISBN-13: 978-1-56097-731-5
First Fantagraphics Books Edition: July 2006

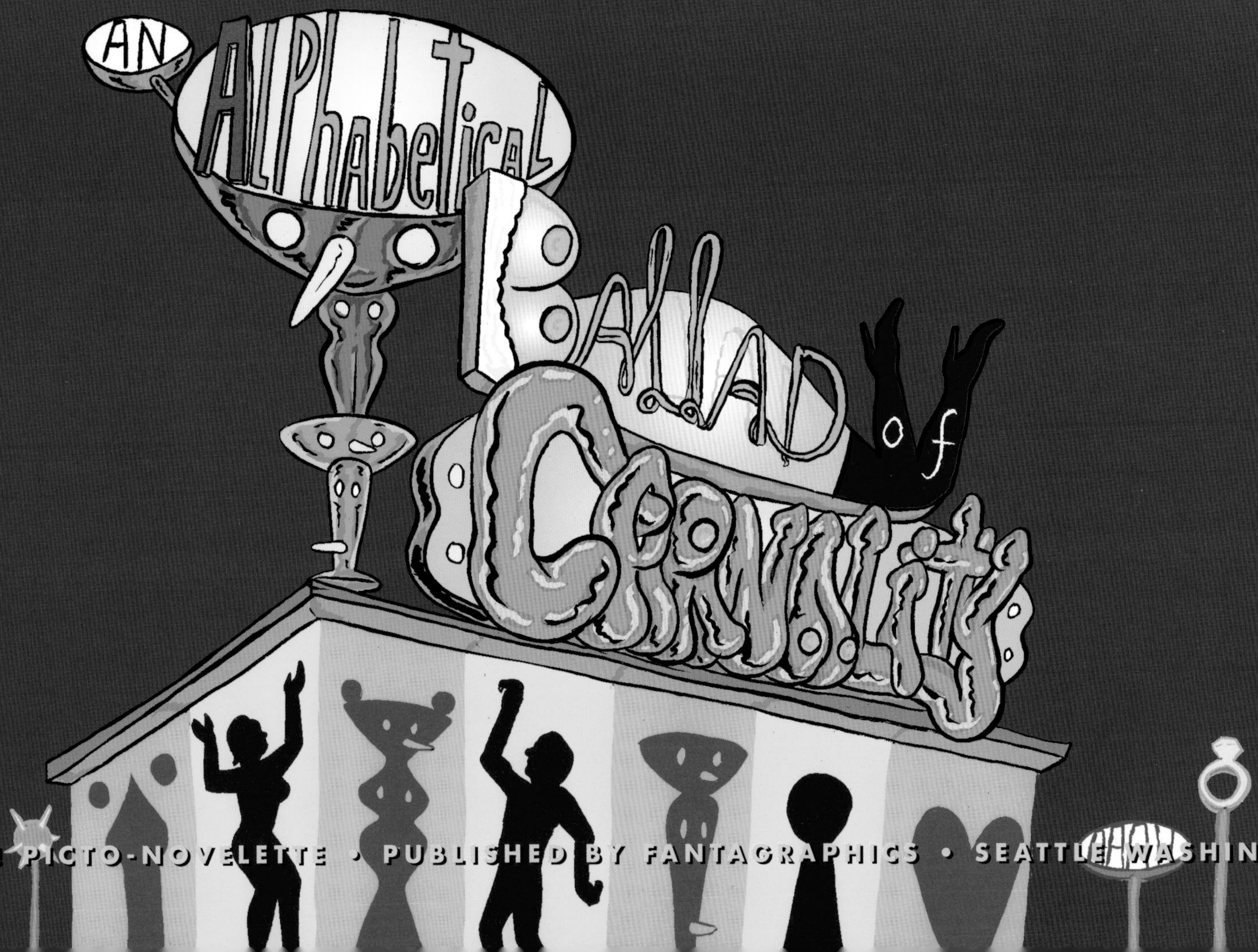
AN
AlPhabetical
BAllAD
of
CARNALITY

A BLAB! PICTO-NOVELETTE • PUBLISHED BY FANTAGRAPHICS • SEATTLE WASHINGTON

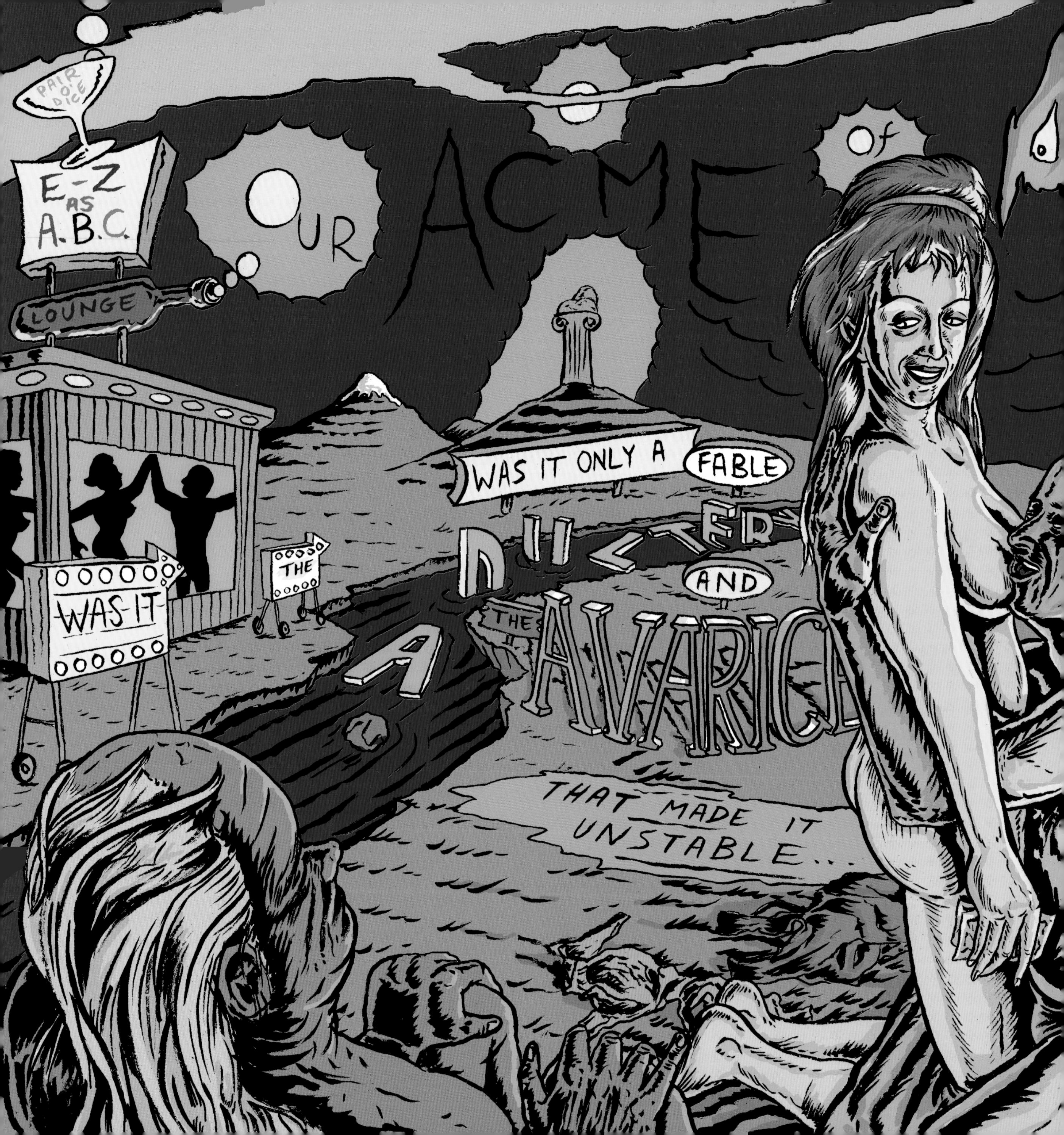

PAIR O' DICE
E-Z AS A.B.C.
LOUNGE
OUR
ACME
OF
WAS IT ONLY A
FABLE
WAS IT
THE
AND
THE
AVARICE
THAT MADE IT UNSTABLE...

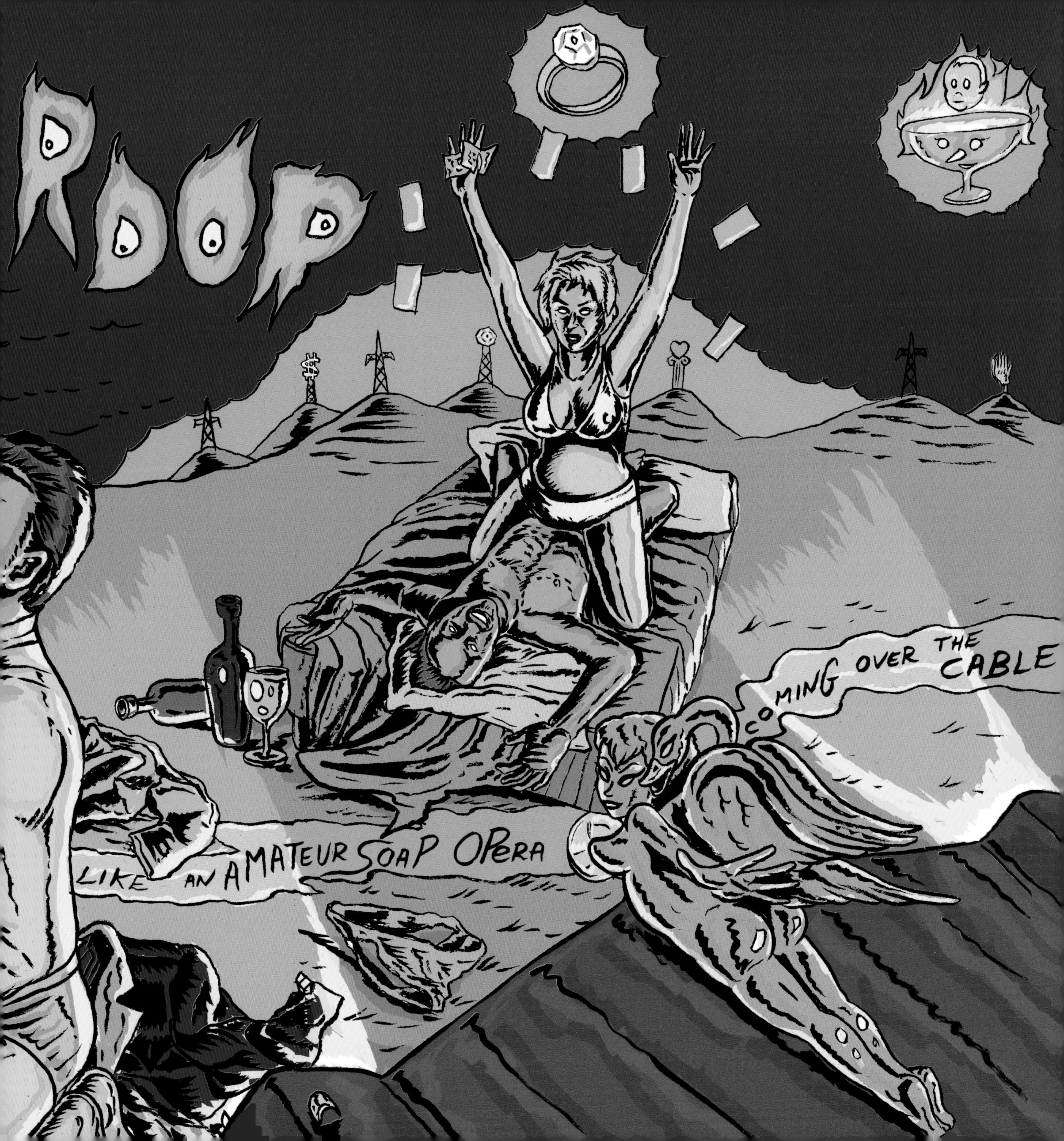

RDOOP
LIKE AN AMATEUR SOAP OPERA
COMING OVER THE CABLE

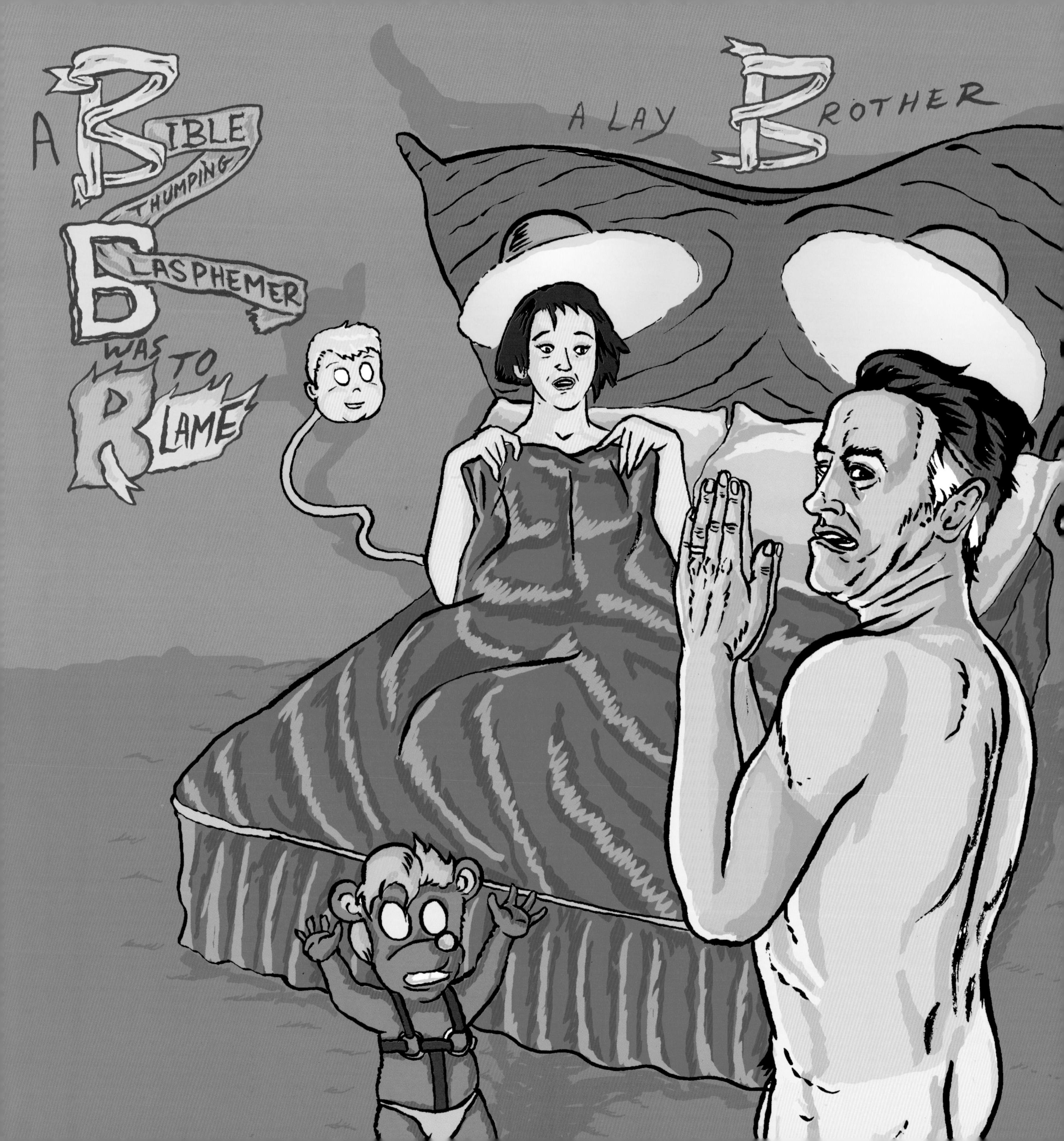
A Bible thumping Blasphemer was to Blame
A Lay Brother

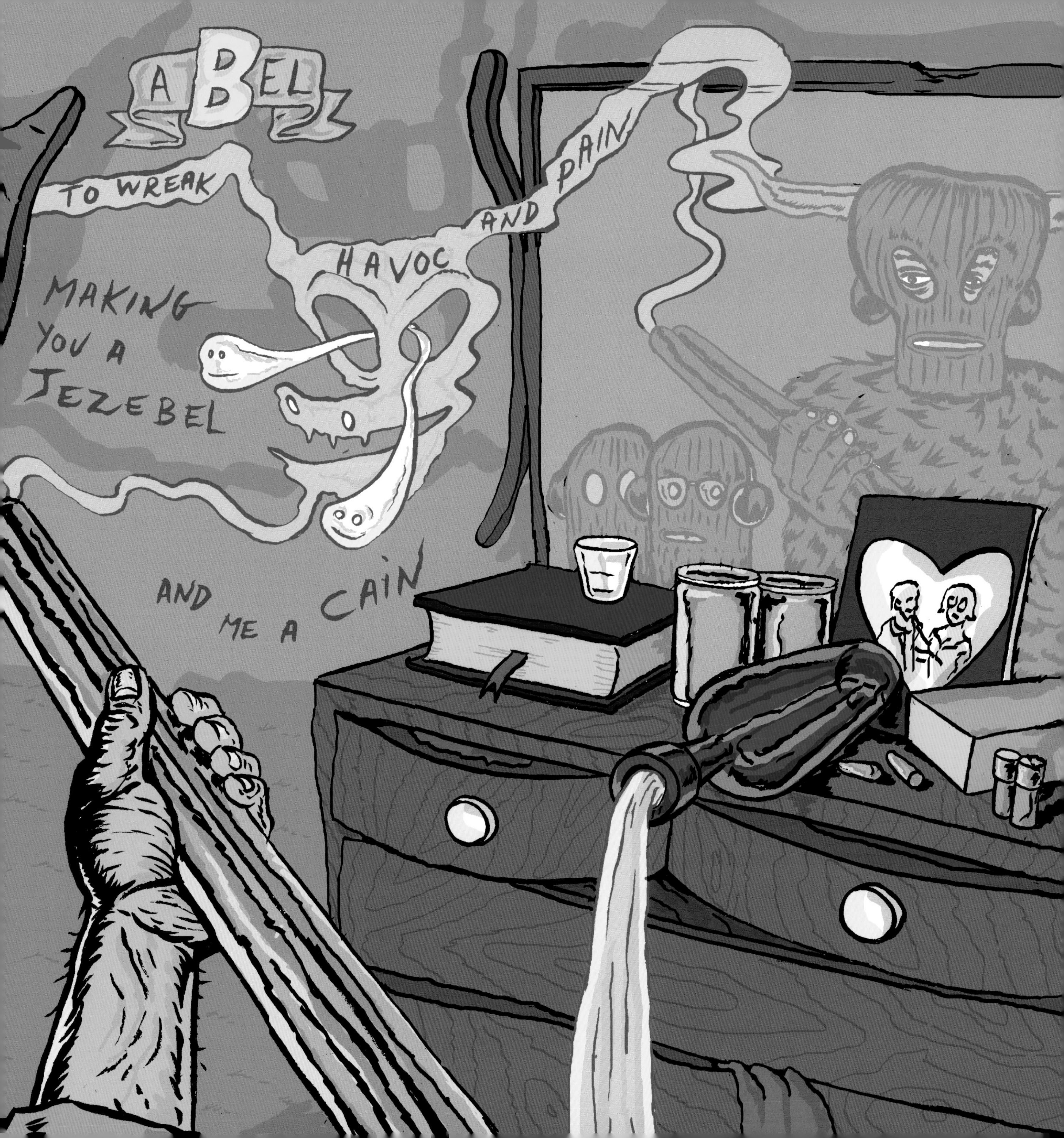
ABEL
TO WREAK HAVOC AND PAIN
MAKING YOU A JEZEBEL
AND ME A CAIN

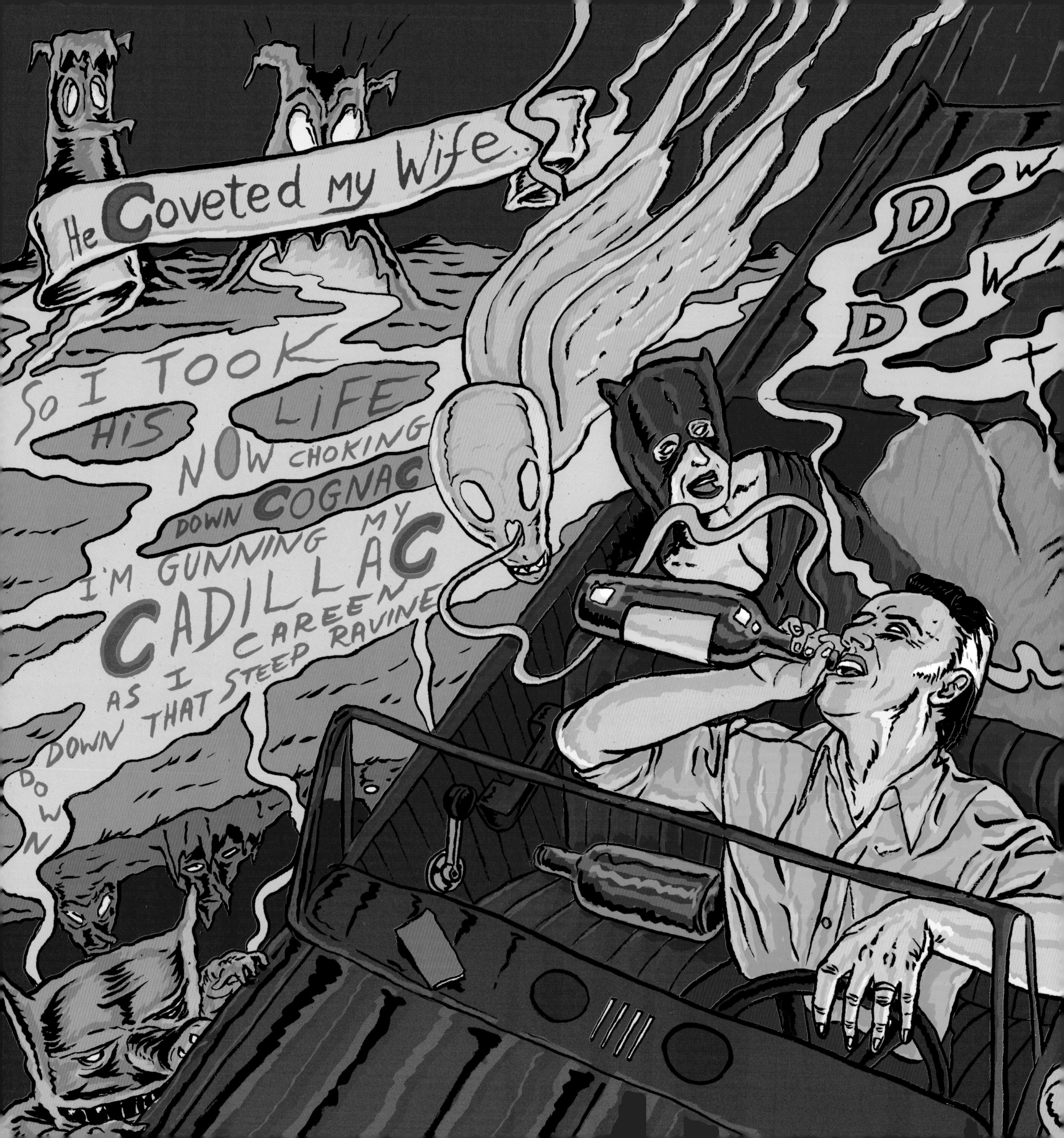
He Coveted my Wife.
So I TOOK HIS LIFE
NOW CHOKING DOWN COGNAC
I'M GUNNING MY CADILLAC
AS I CAREEN DOWN THAT STEEP RAVINE
DOWN DOWN
DOWN DOWN DOWN

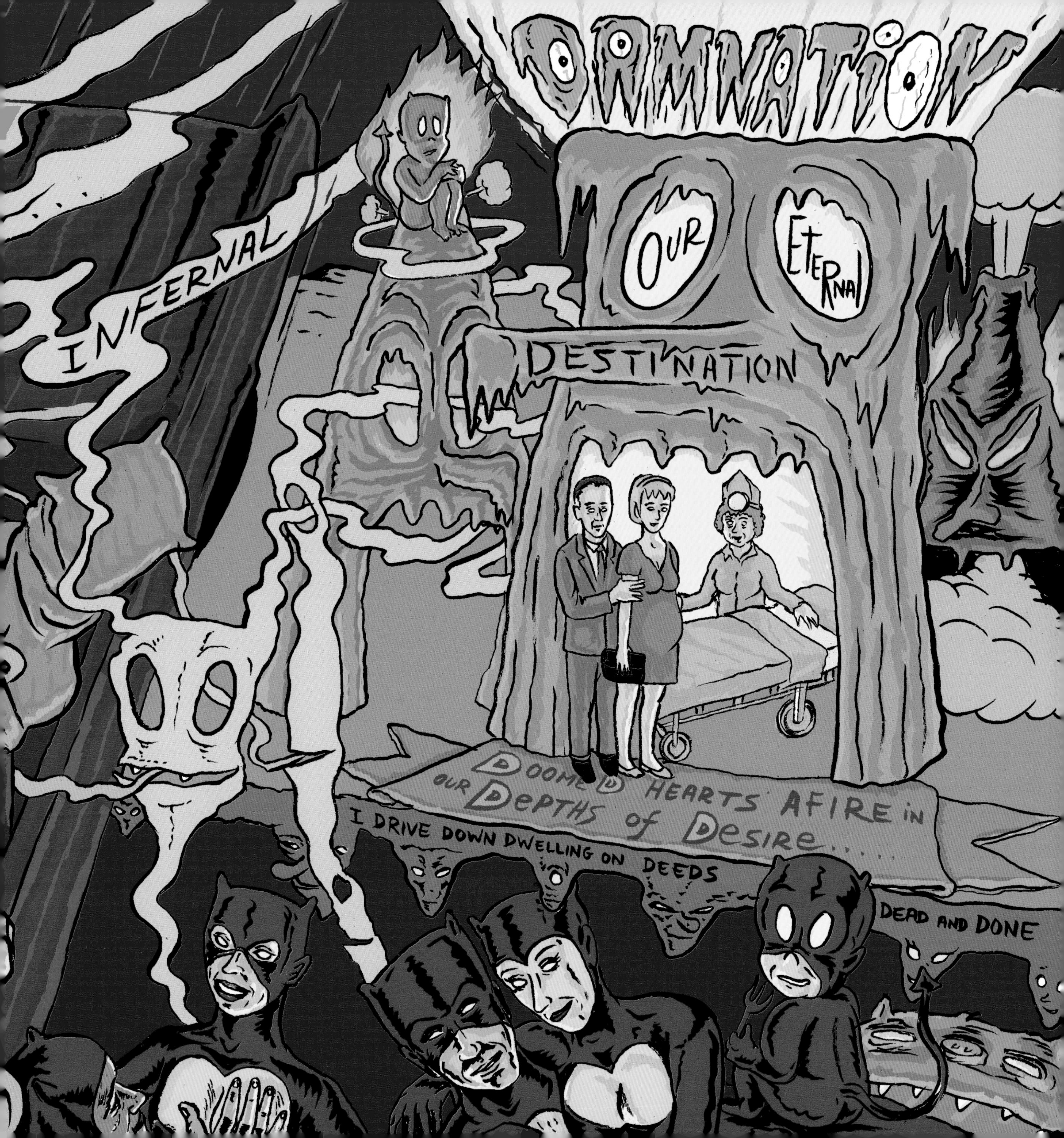
DAMNATION
INFERNAL
OUR
ETERNAL
DESTINATION
DOOMED HEARTS AFIRE IN OUR DEPTHS OF DESIRE...
I DRIVE DOWN DWELLING ON DEEDS
DEAD AND DONE

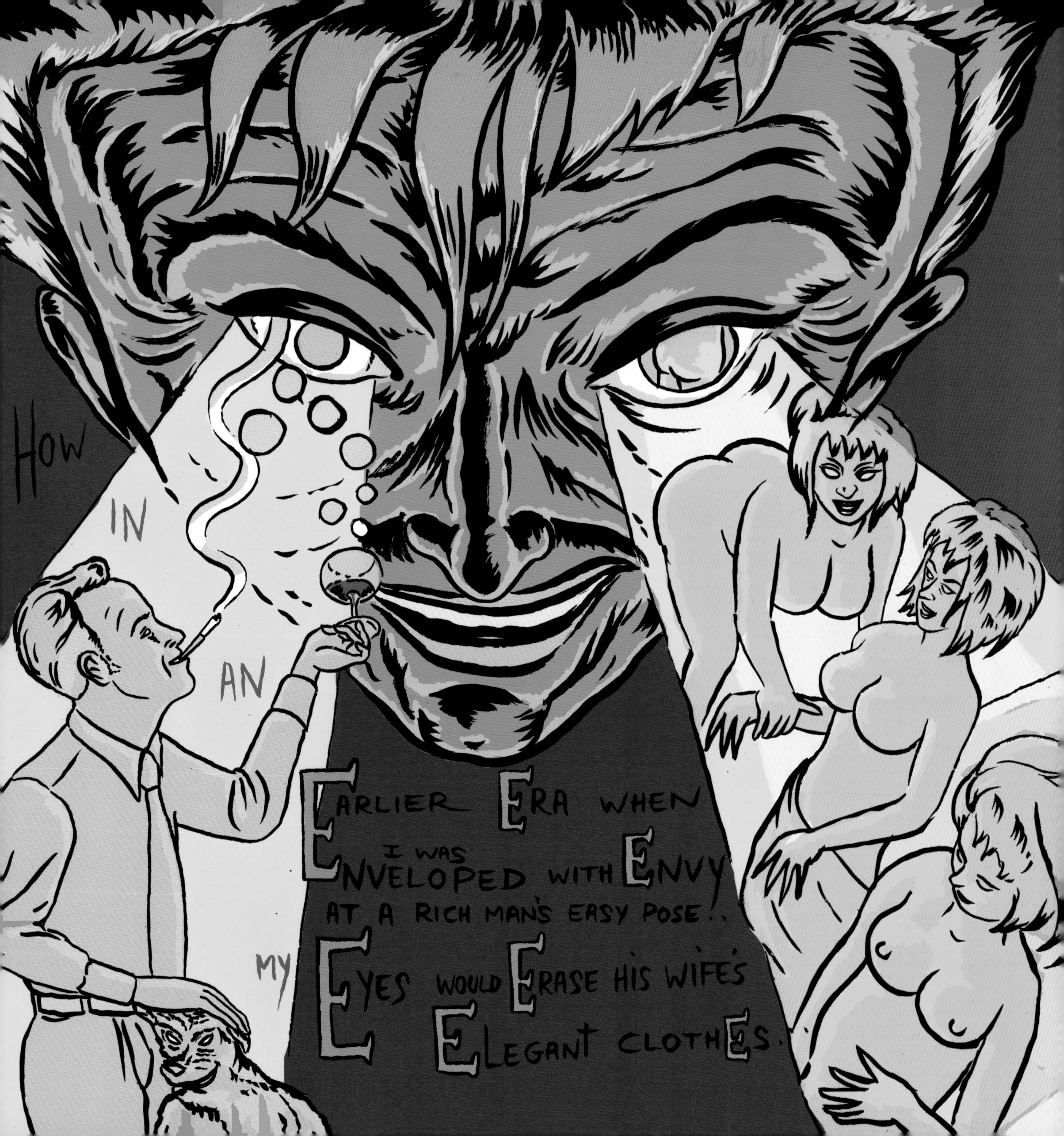
HOW
IN
AN
EARLIER ERA WHEN
I WAS
ENVELOPED WITH ENVY
AT A RICH MAN'S EASY POSE..
MY EYES WOULD ERASE HIS WIFE'S
ELEGANT CLOTHES.

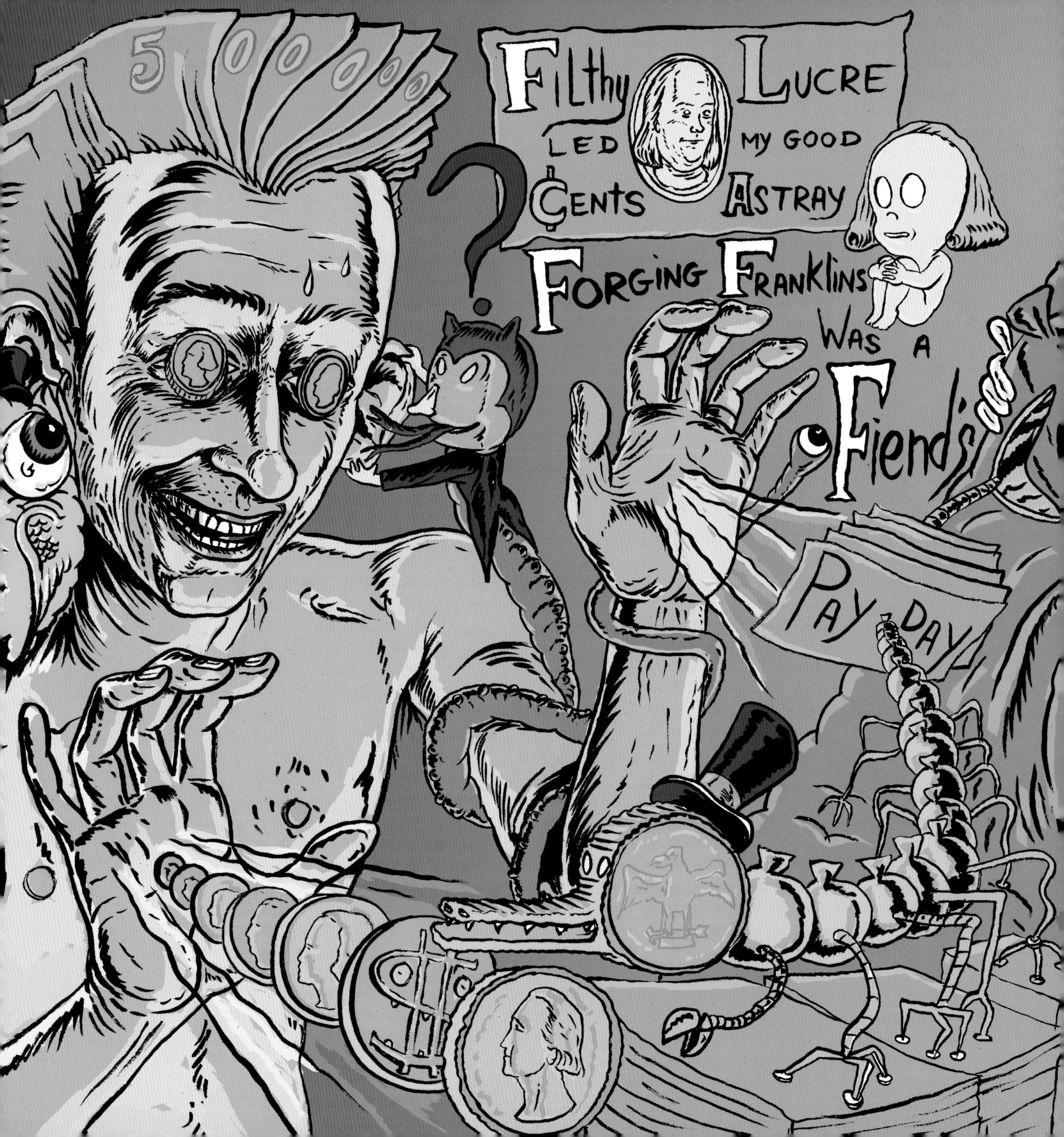

Filthy Lucre
Led my good
Cents Astray
Forging Franklins Was a Fiend's
Pay Day

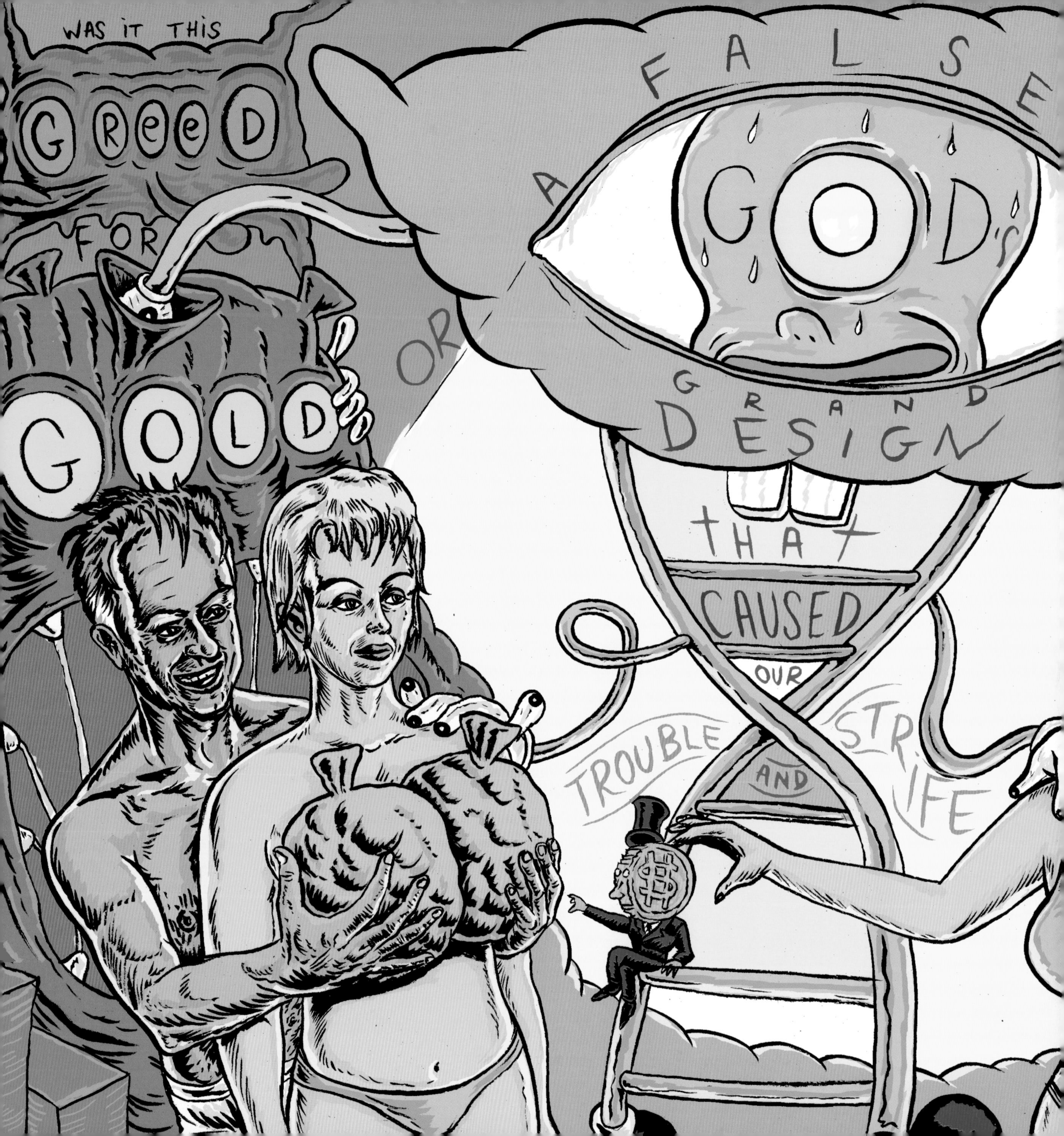
WAS IT THIS
GREED
FOR
GOLD
OR
A FALSE
GOD'S
GRAND
DESIGN
THAT
CAUSED
OUR
TROUBLE
AND
STRIFE

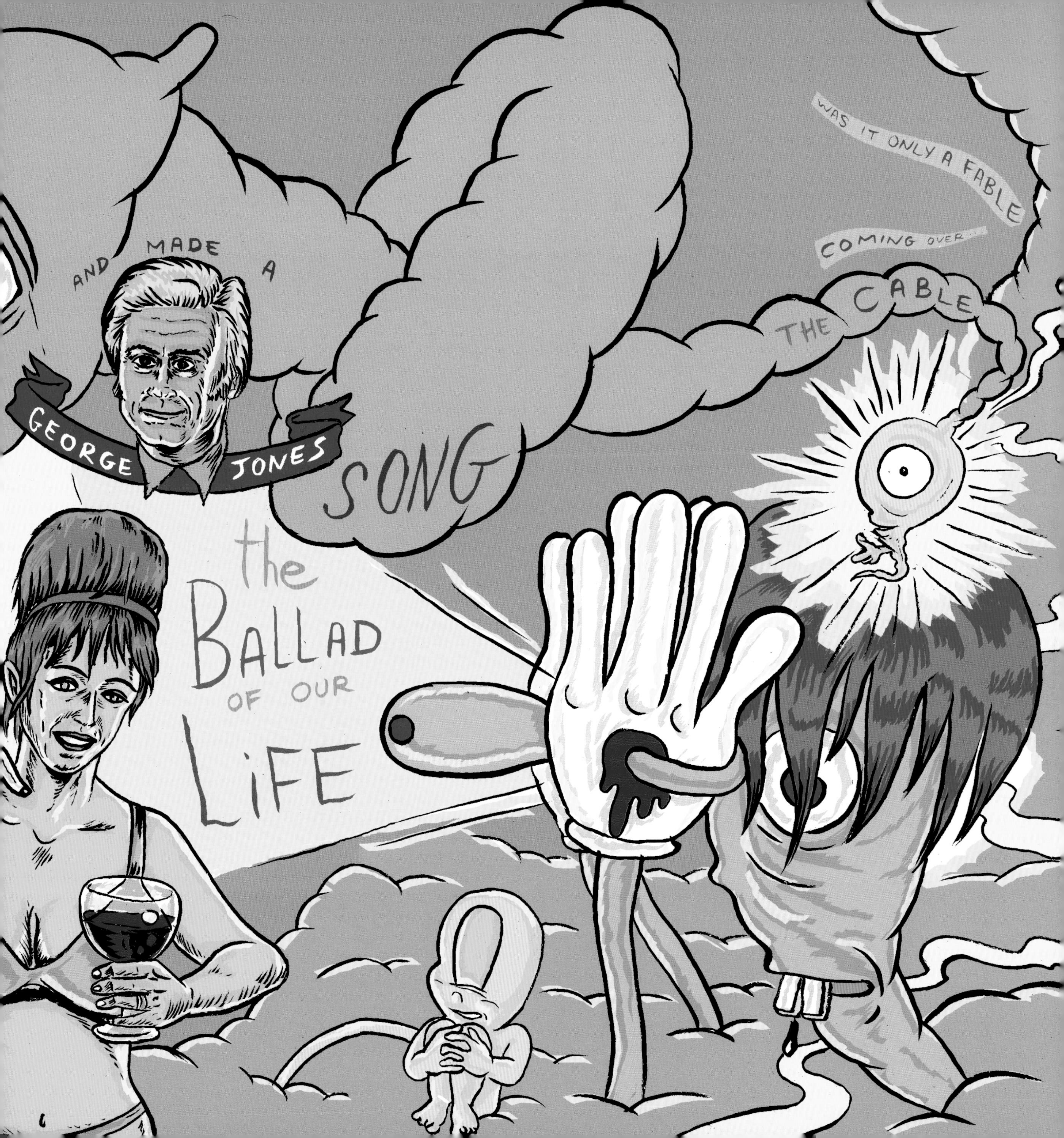
AND MADE A
GEORGE JONES
SONG
WAS IT ONLY A FABLE
COMING OVER...
THE CABLE
the BALLAD OF OUR LiFE

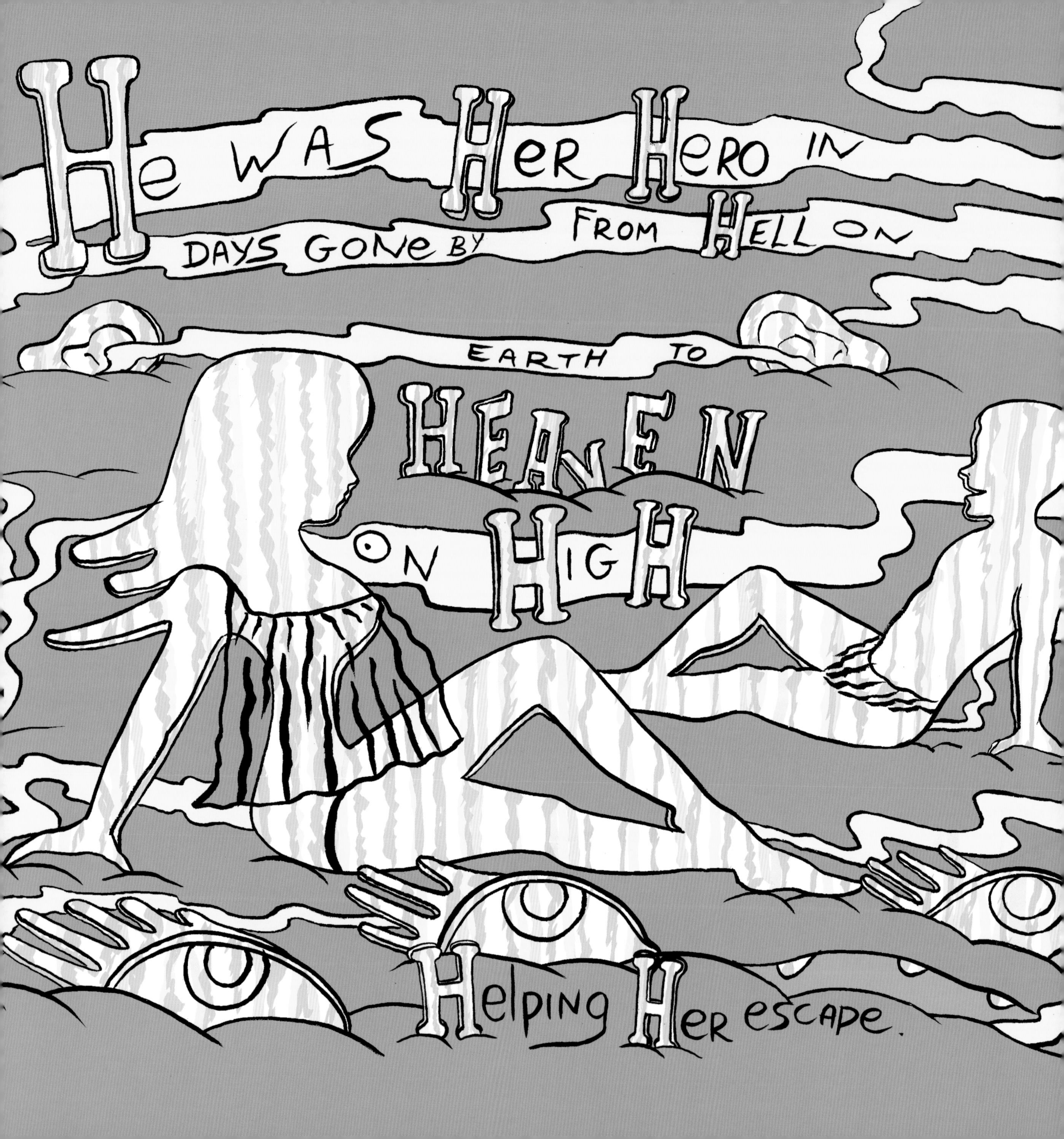
He was Her Hero in
days gone by
from Hell on
earth to
Heaven
on High
Helping Her escape.

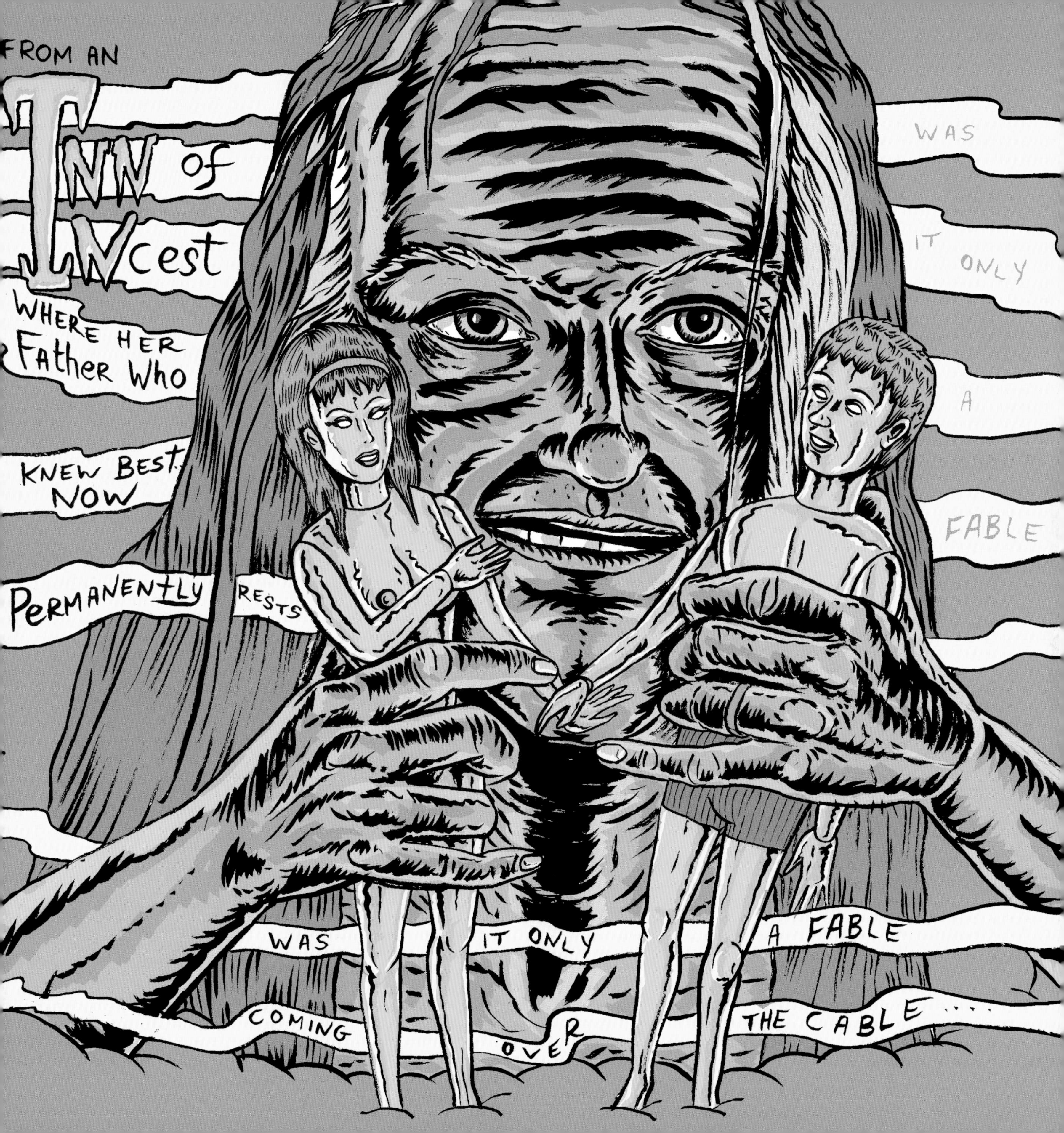
FROM AN
INN of INcest
WHERE HER Father Who
KNEW BEST. NOW
PERMANENTLY RESTS
WAS
IT ONLY
A
FABLE
WAS IT ONLY A FABLE
COMING OVER THE CABLE....

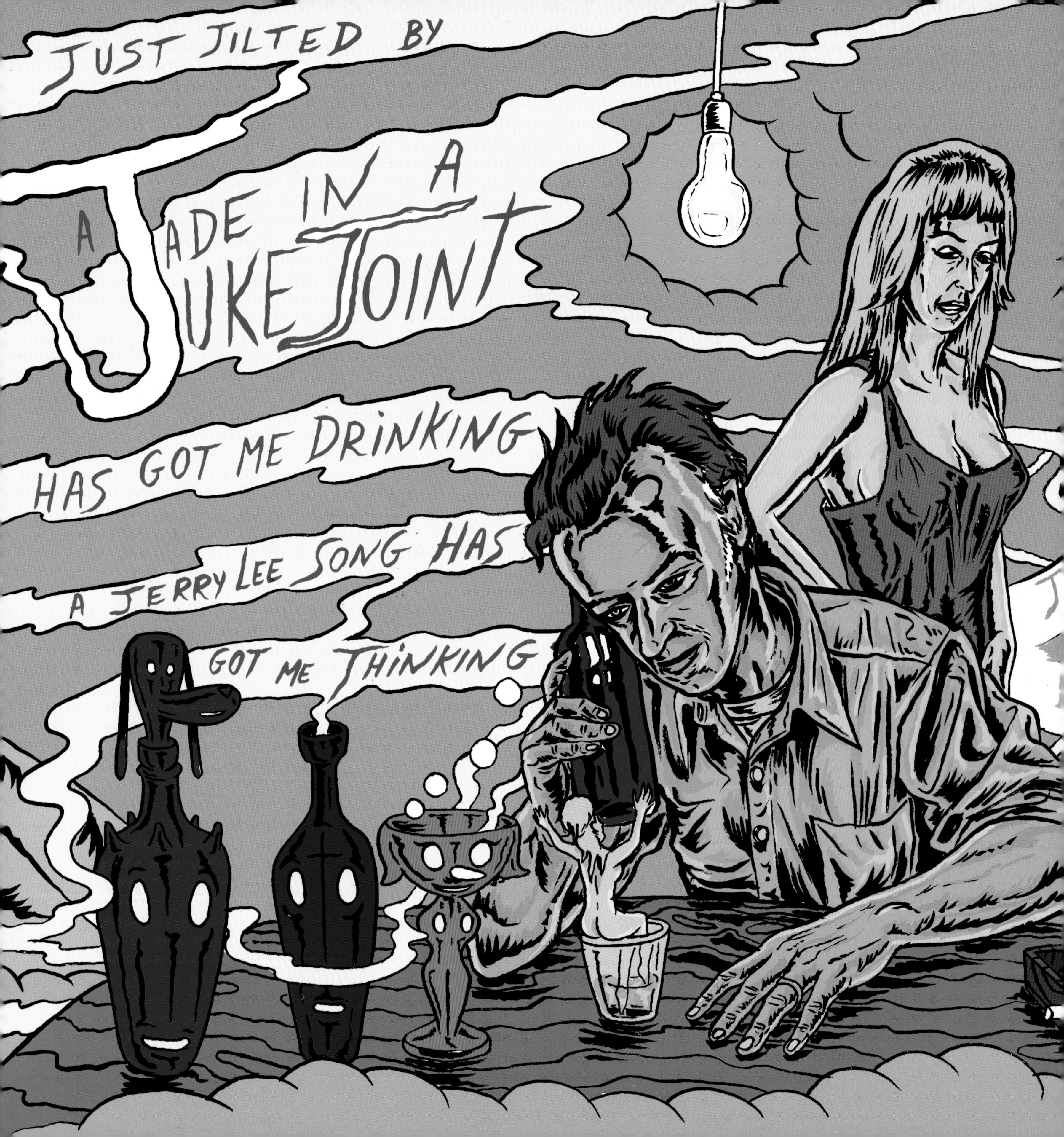
JUST JILTED BY
A JADE IN A JUKE JOINT
HAS GOT ME DRINKING
A JERRY LEE SONG HAS
GOT ME THINKING

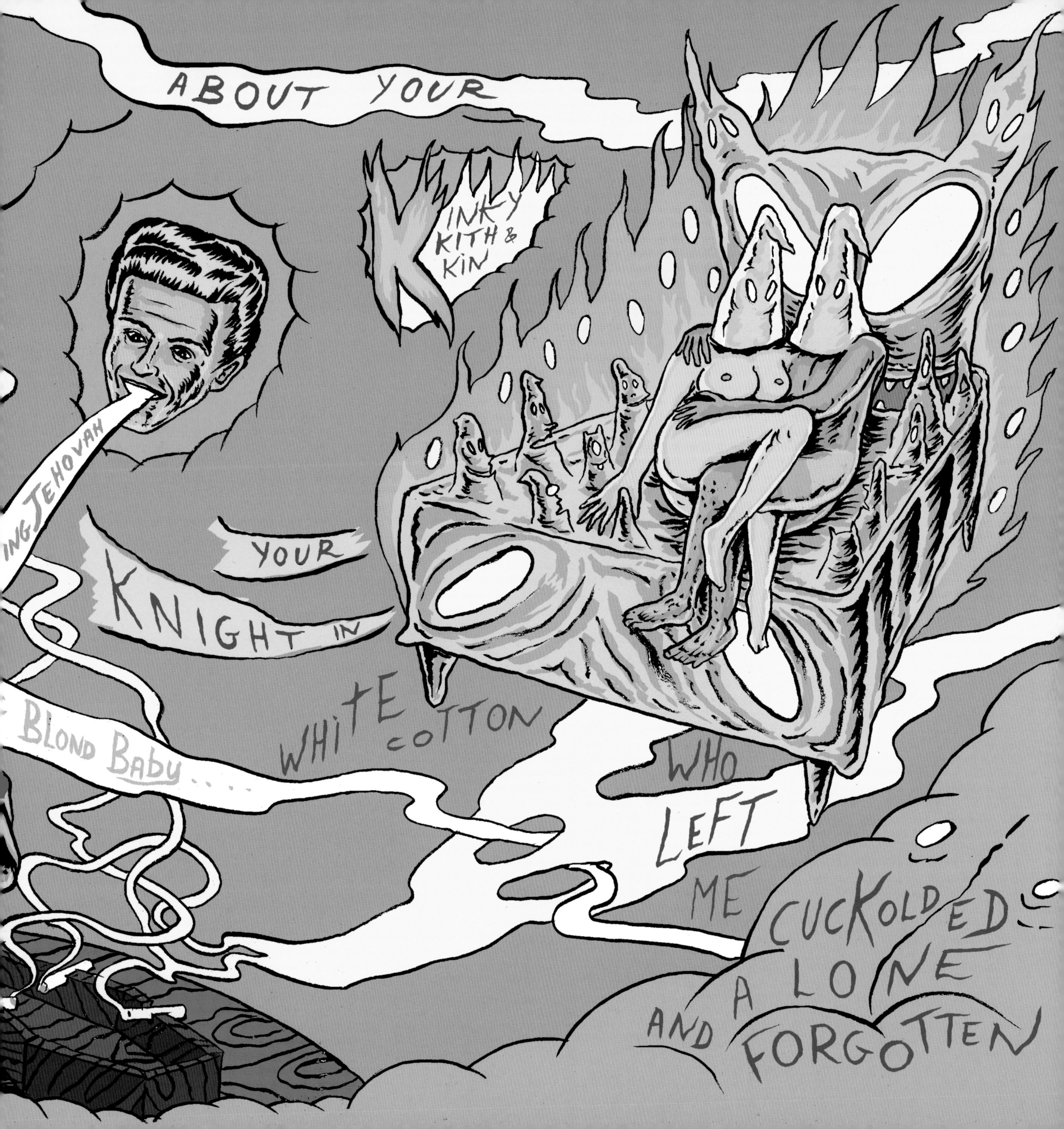

ABOUT YOUR
KINKY KITH & KIN
ING JEHOVAH
YOUR
KNIGHT IN
WHITE COTTON
BLOND BABY....
WHO LEFT ME
CUCKOLDED
ALONE
AND FORGOTTEN

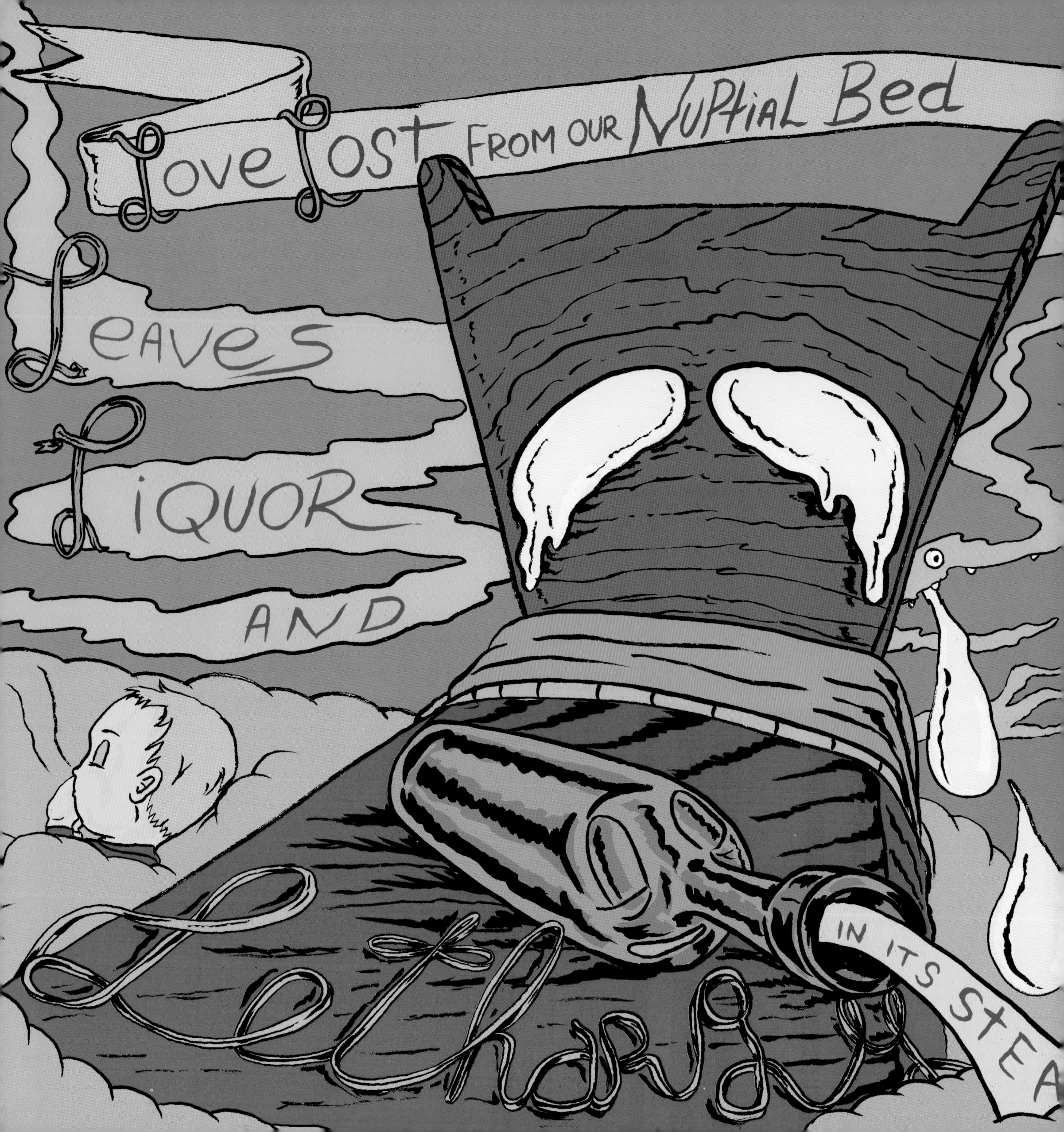
Love Lost from our Nuptial Bed
Leaves
Liquor
and
Lethargy
in its stead

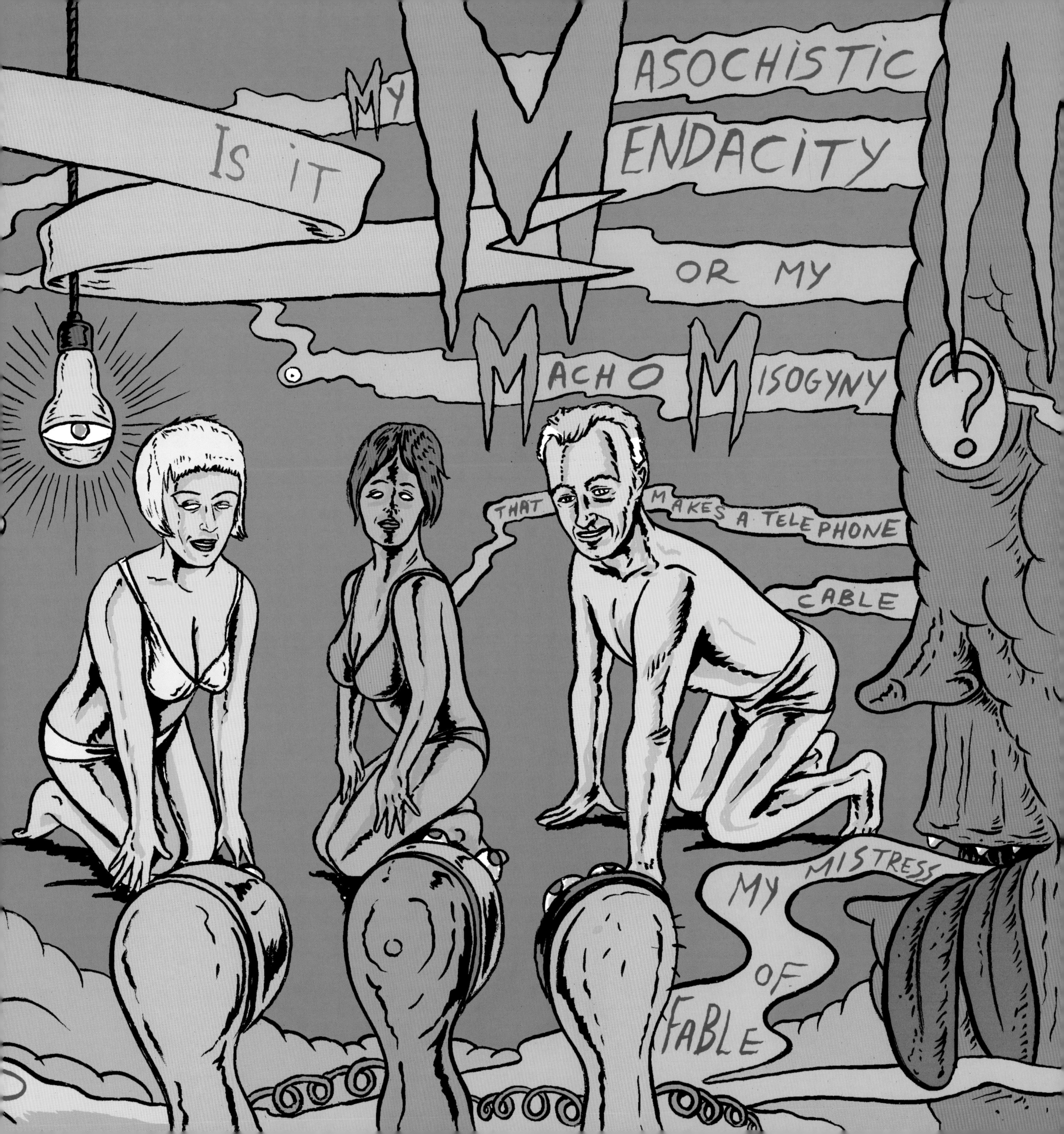
Is it My Masochistic Mendacity
or my Macho Misogyny
that makes a telephone cable
My mistress of fable

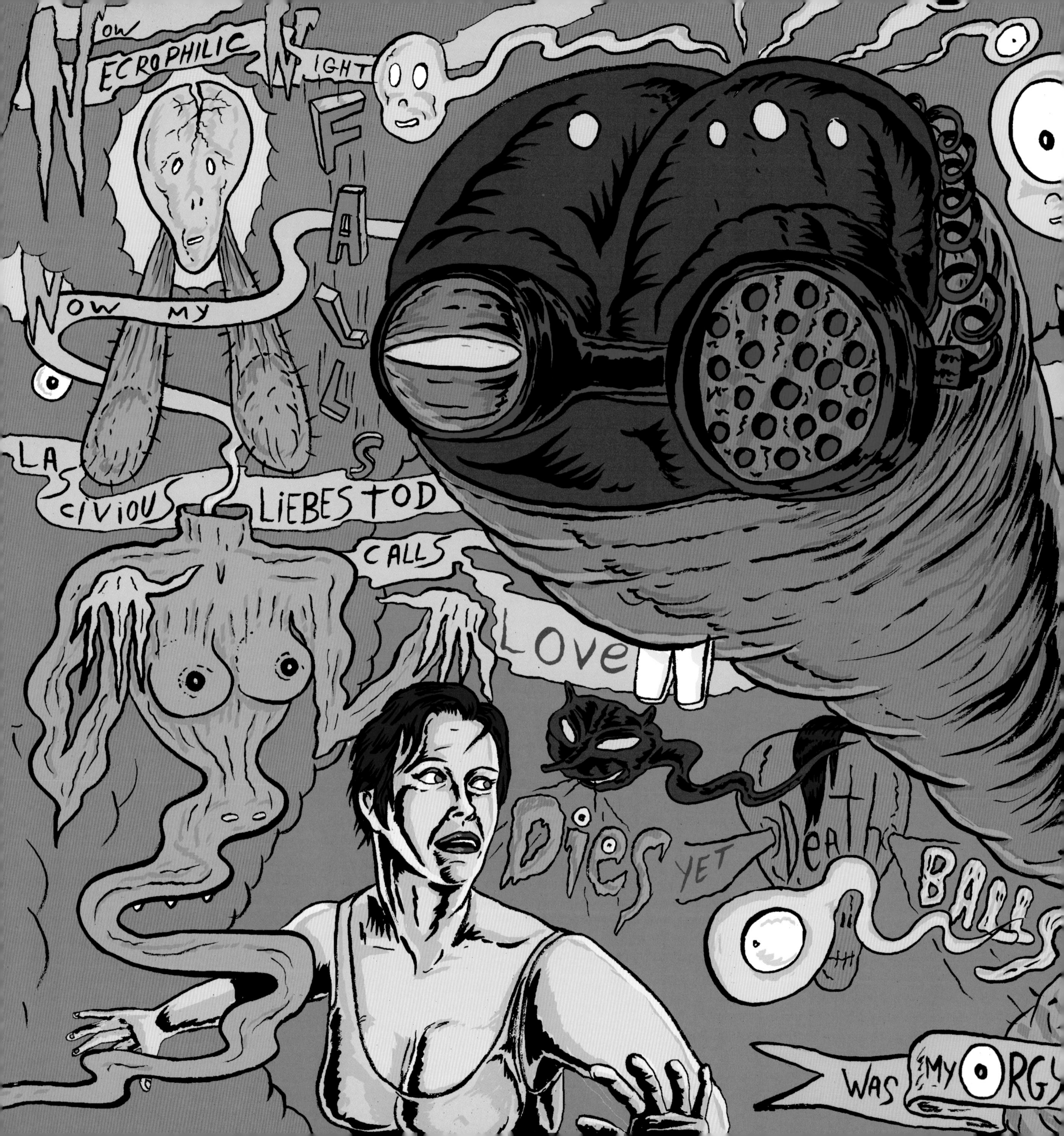
NOW NECROPHILIC NIGHT
FALLS
NOW MY
LASCIVIOUS LIEBESTOD
CALLS
LOVE
DIES YET DEATH
BALLS
WAS MY ORGY

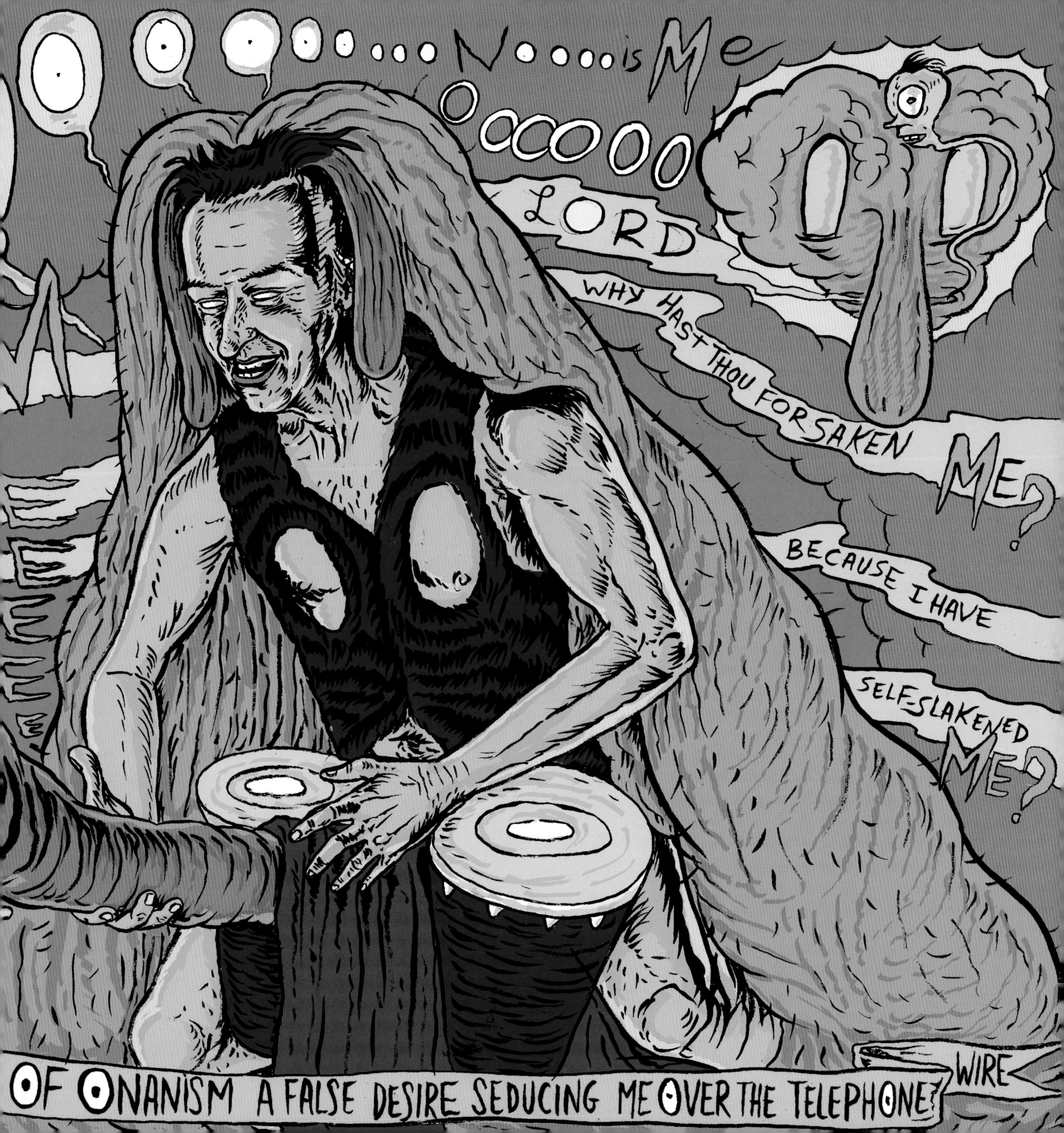
O O O O o o o . . . N o o o o . . . is Me
OOCOOO
LORD
WHY HAST THOU FORSAKEN ME?
BECAUSE I HAVE SELF-SLAKENED ME?
OF ONANISM A FALSE DESIRE SEDUCING ME OVER THE TELEPHONE WIRE

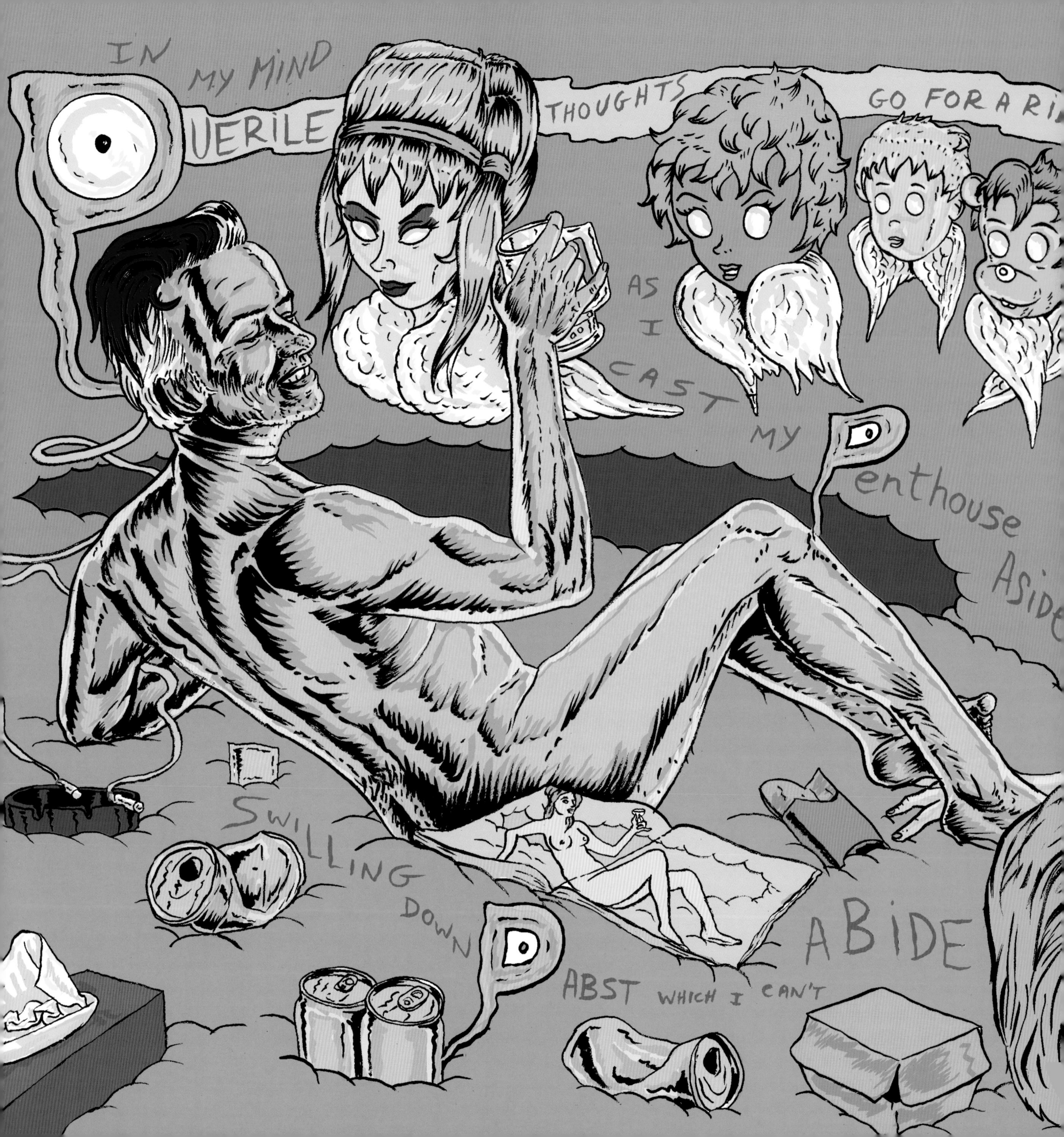
IN MY MIND
PUERILE THOUGHTS GO FOR A RI
AS I CAST MY PENTHOUSE ASIDE
SWILLING DOWN PABST WHICH I CAN'T ABIDE

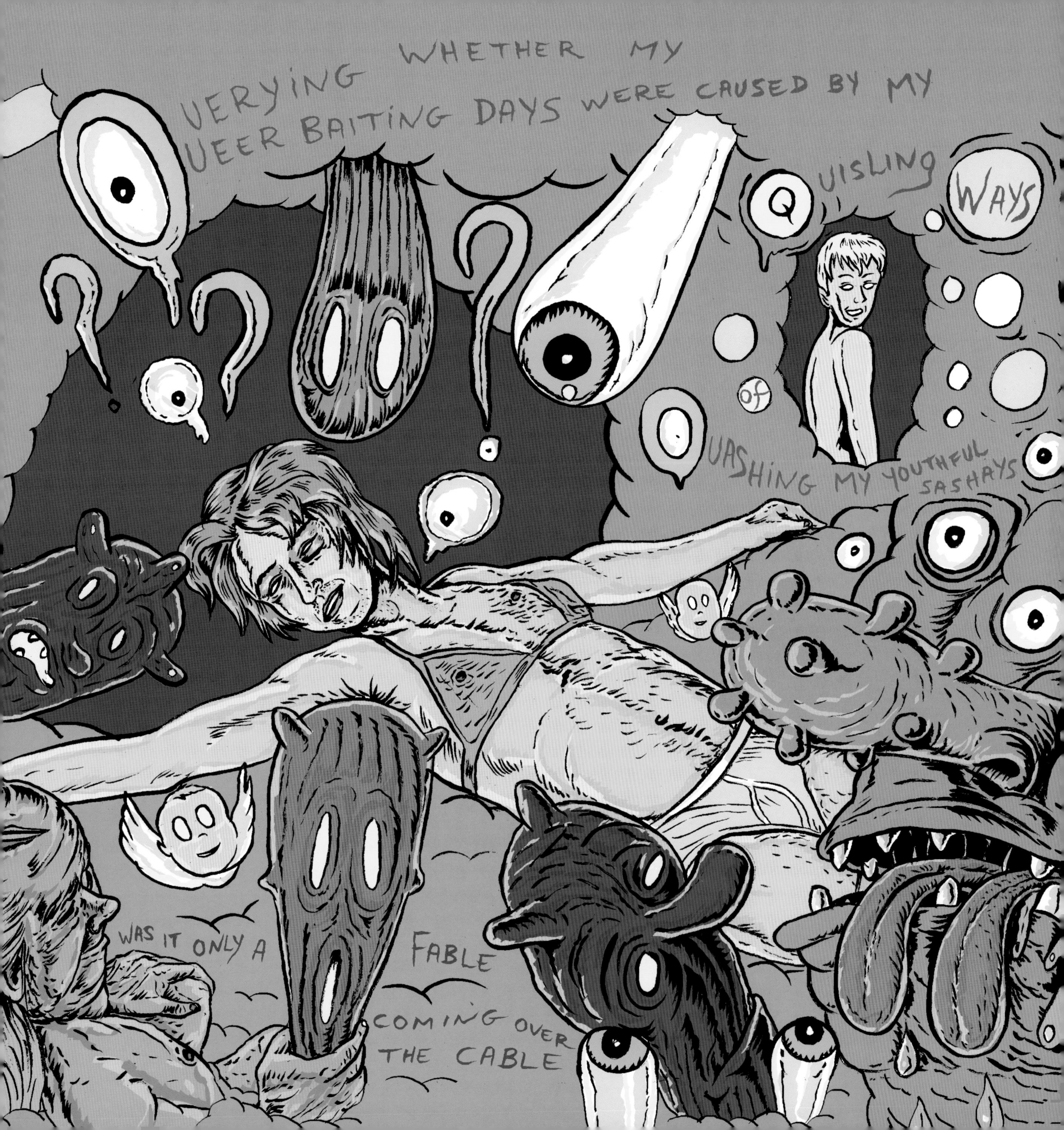

WHETHER MY
UERYING
UEER BAITING DAYS WERE CAUSED BY MY
Q UISLING WAYS
of
UASHING MY YOUTHFUL SASHAYS
WAS IT ONLY A
FABLE
COMING OVER THE CABLE

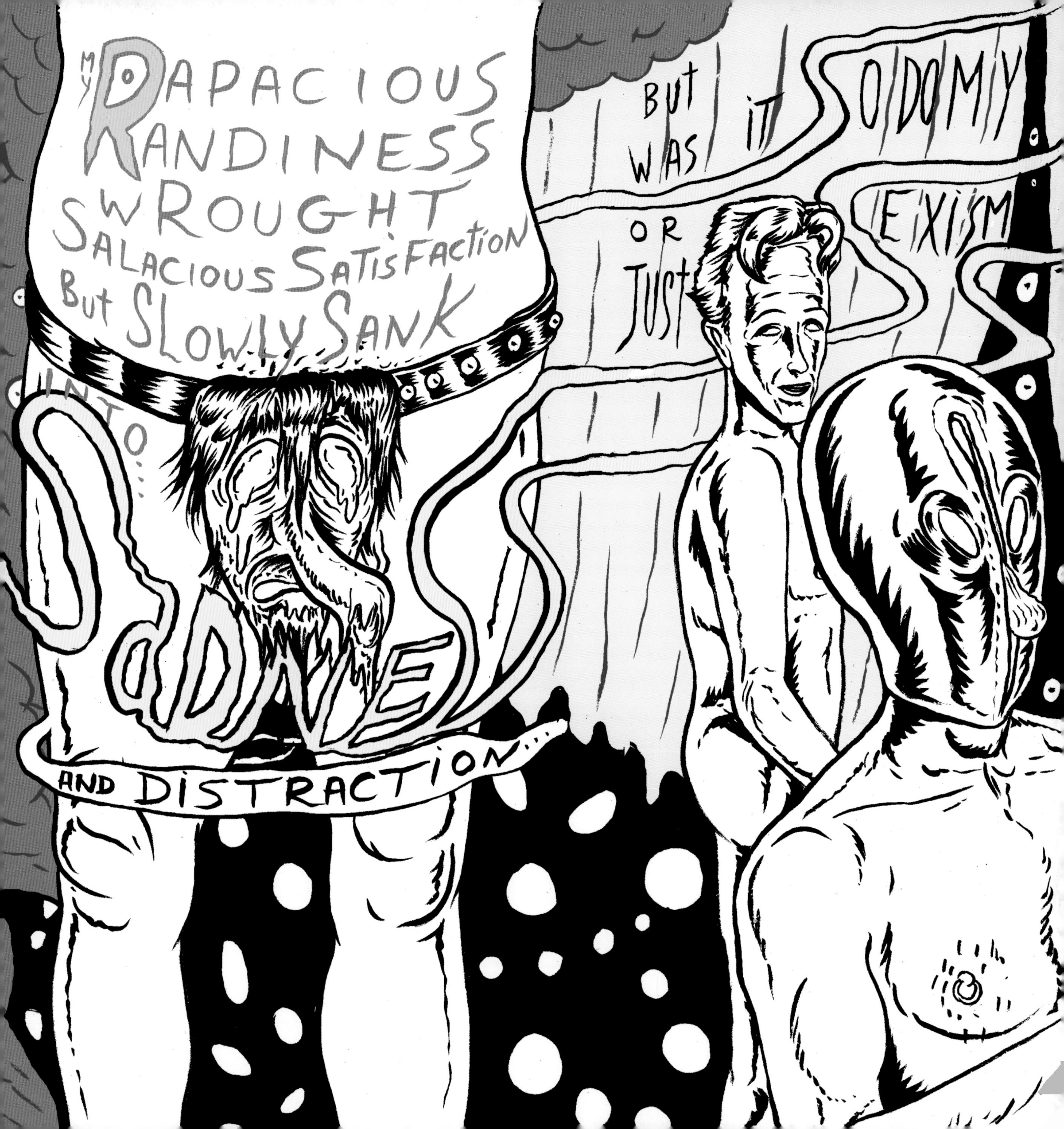

MY RAPACIOUS RANDINESS WROUGHT SALACIOUS SATISFACTION BUT SLOWLY SANK INTO SADNESS AND DISTRACTION
BUT WAS IT SODOMY OR JUST SEXISM

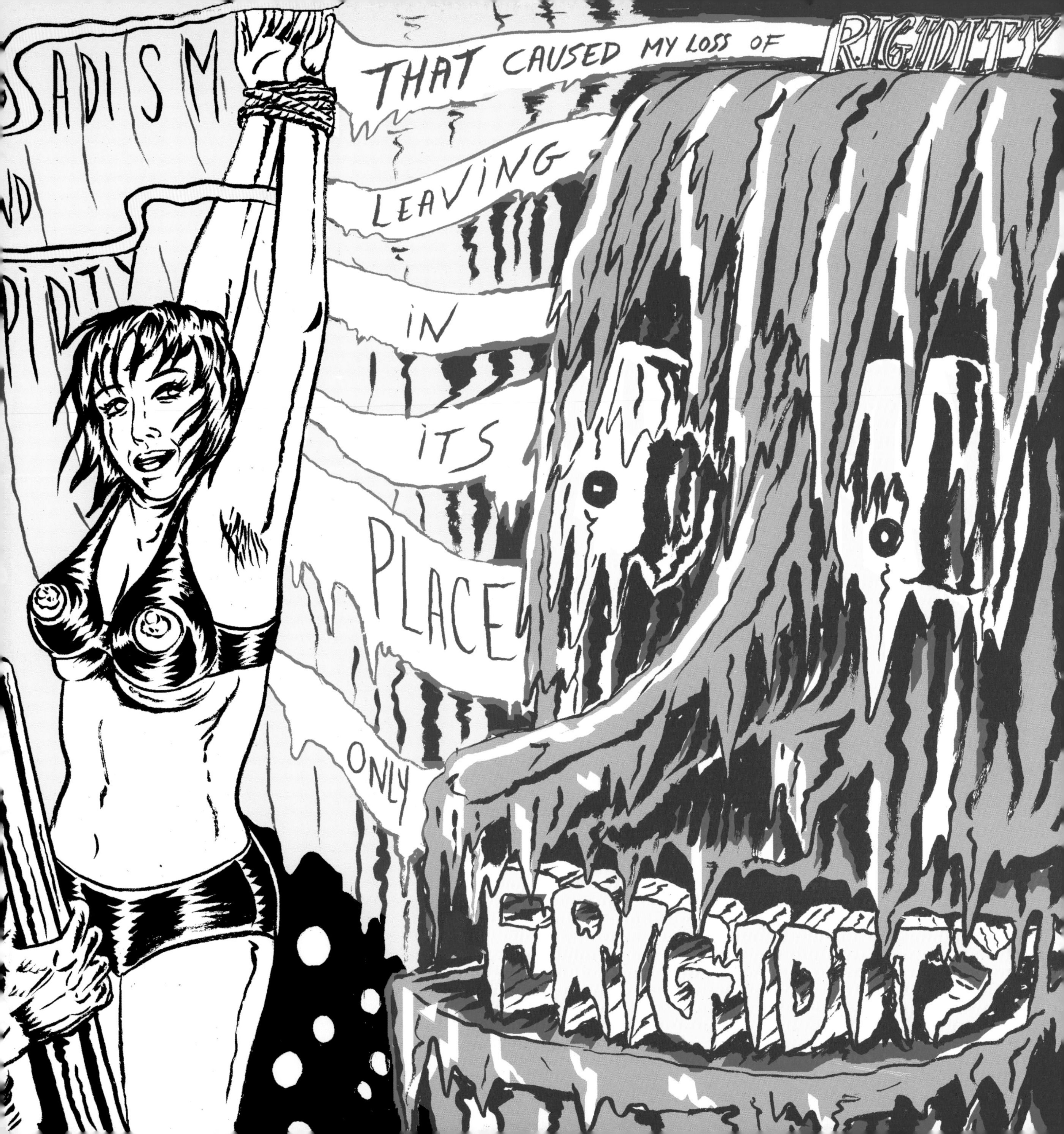
SADISM
ND
PIDITY
THAT CAUSED MY LOSS OF
RIGIDITY
LEAVING
IN
ITS
PLACE
ONLY
FRIGIDITY

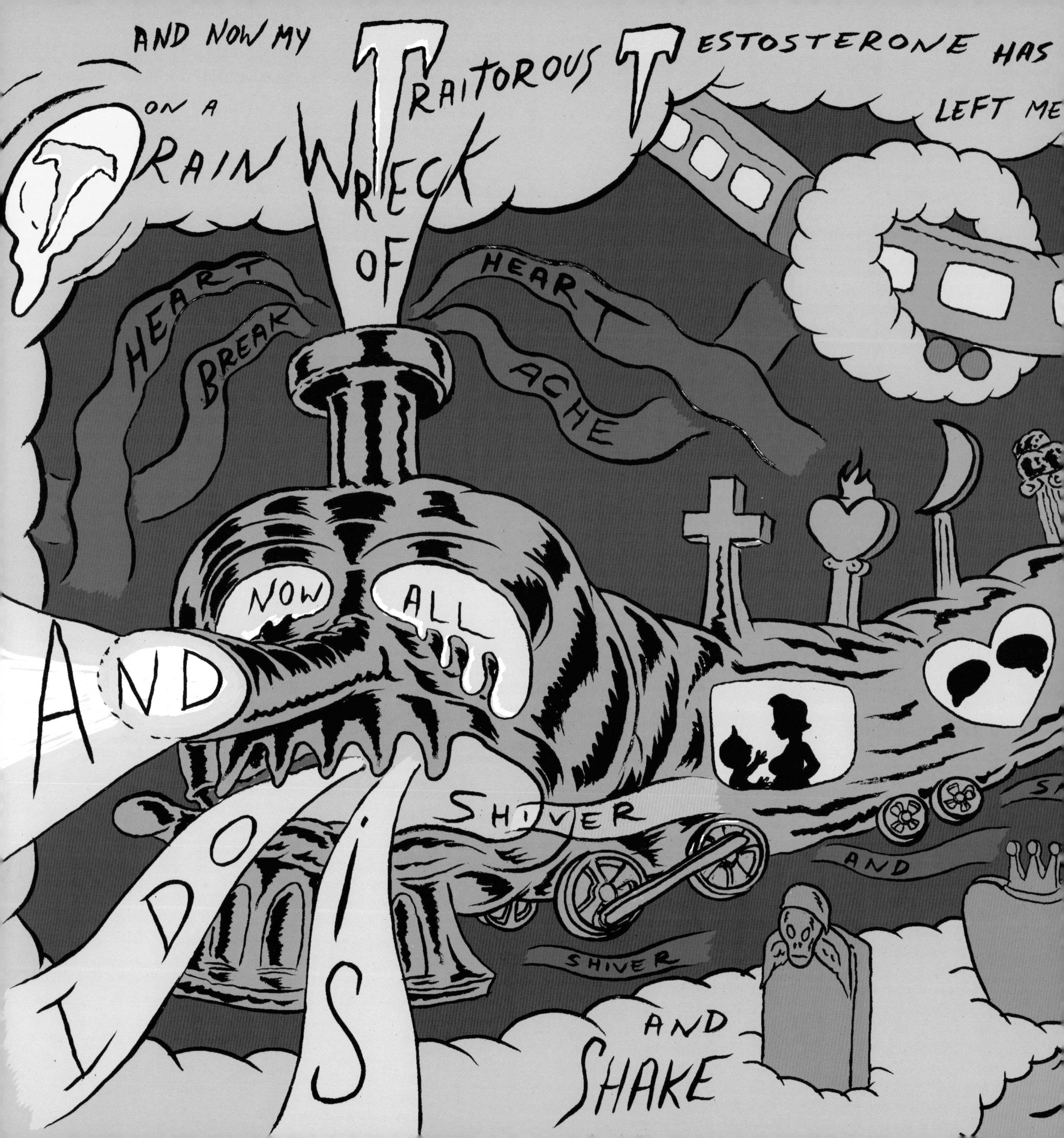
AND NOW MY TRAITOROUS TESTOSTERONE HAS LEFT ME
ON A TRAIN WRECK OF
HEART BREAK
HEART ACHE
AND NOW ALL I DO IS
SHIVER
AND
SHIVER
AND SHAKE

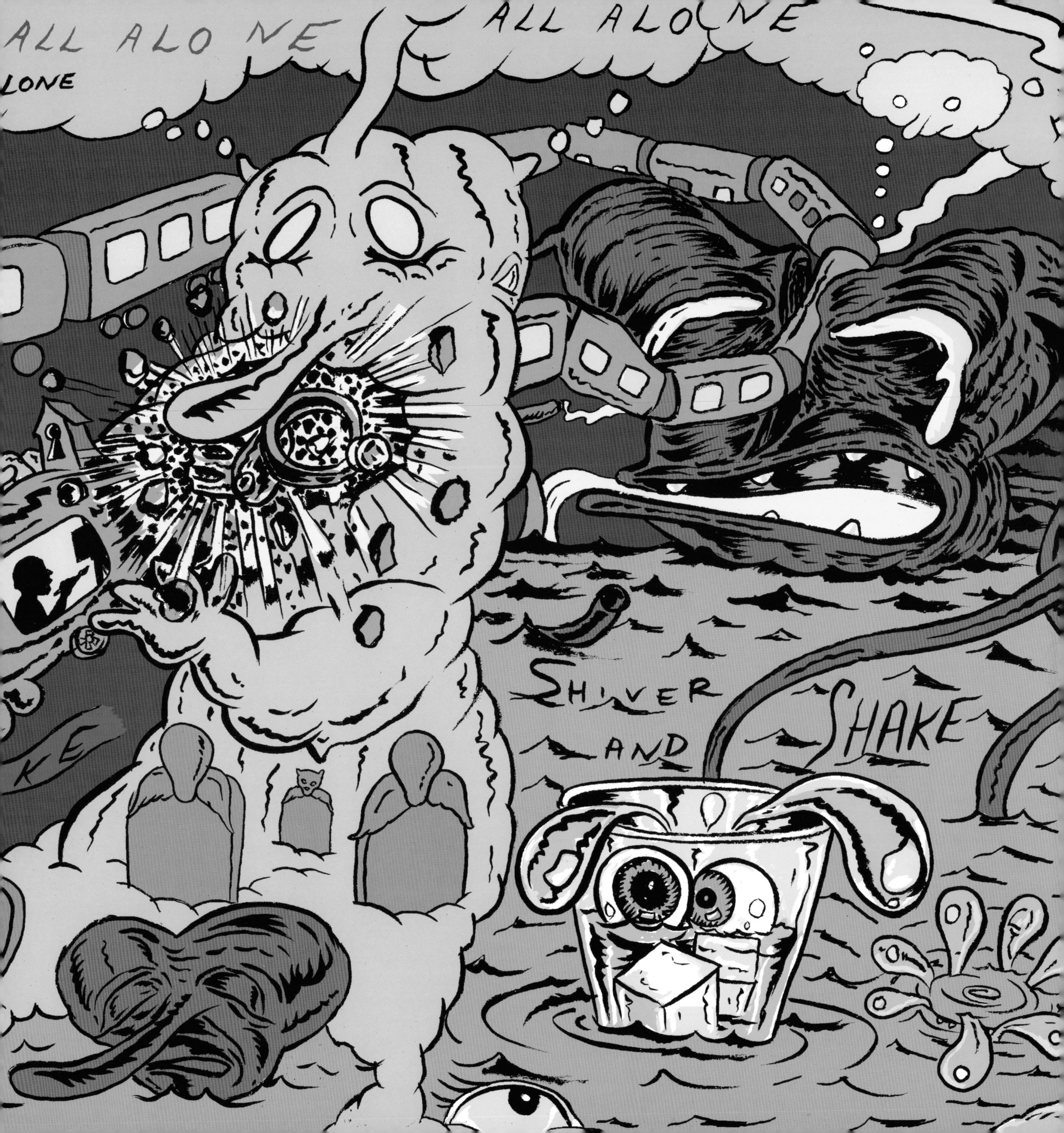
ALL ALONE
LONE
ALL ALONE
SHIVER
AND
SHAKE
KE

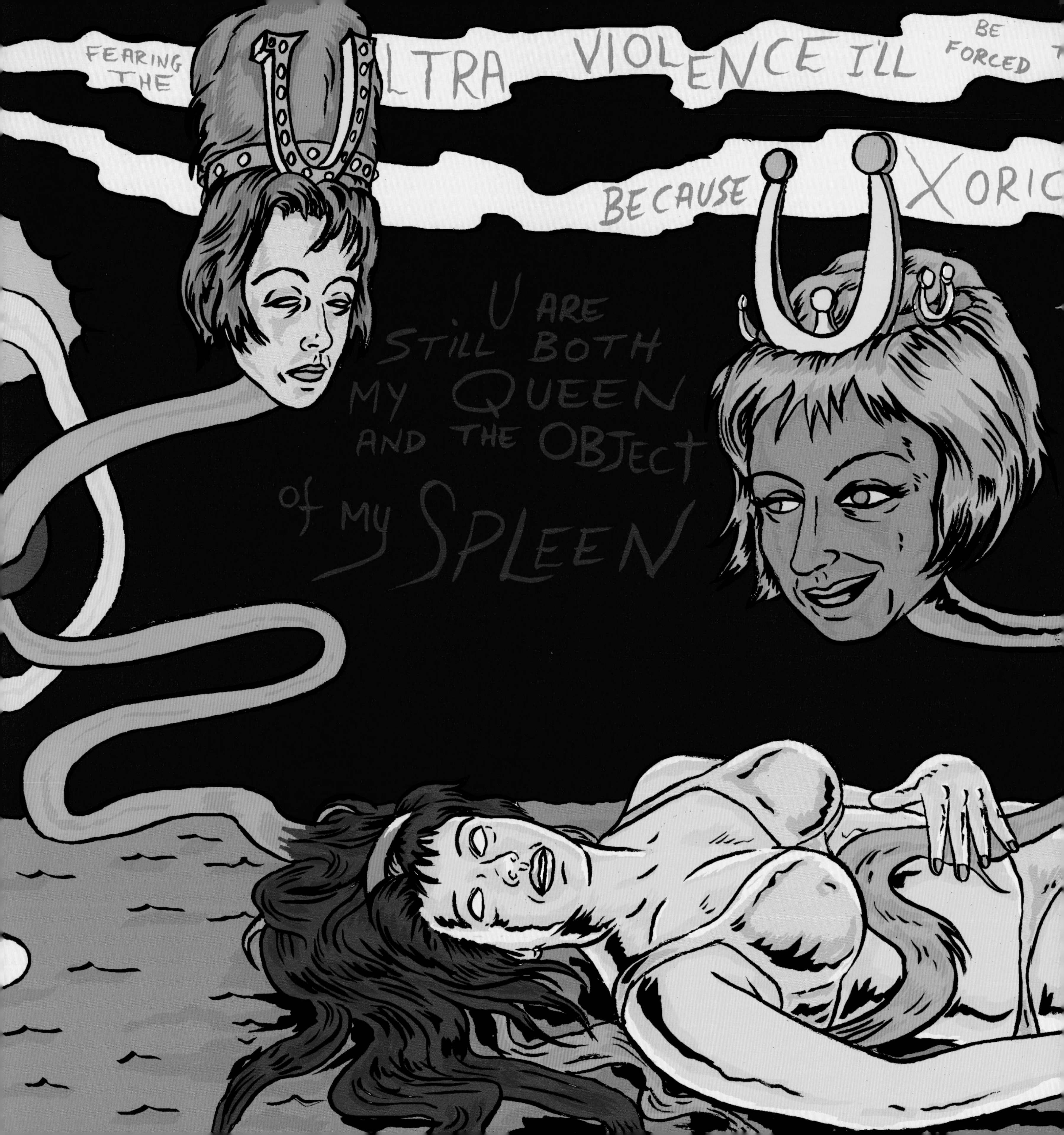
FEARING THE ULTRA VIOLENCE I'LL BE FORCED T
BECAUSE U XORIC
U ARE STILL BOTH MY QUEEN AND THE OBJECT of MY SPLEEN

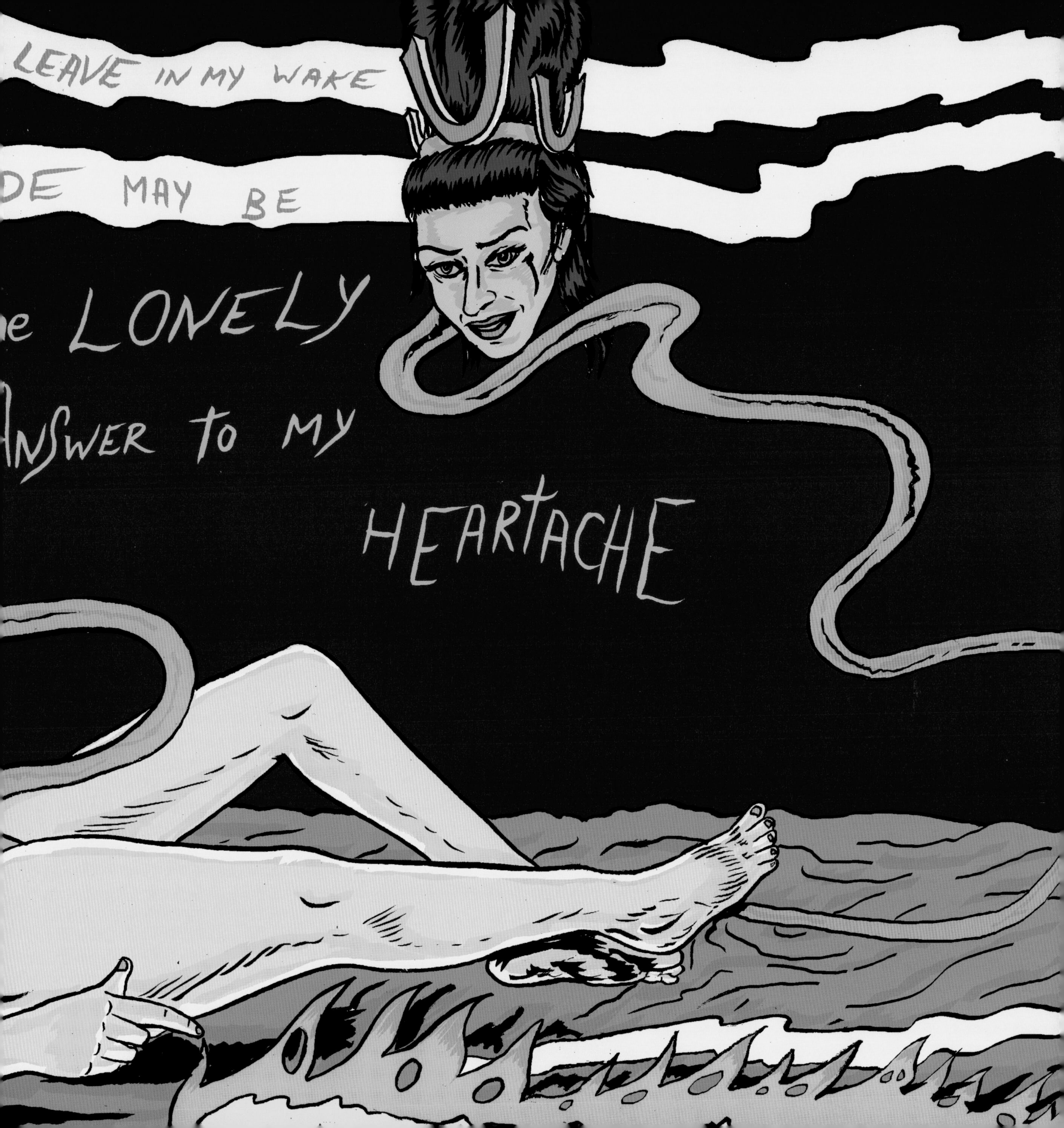
LEAVE IN MY WAKE
DE MAY BE
e LONELY
NSWER TO MY
HEARTACHE

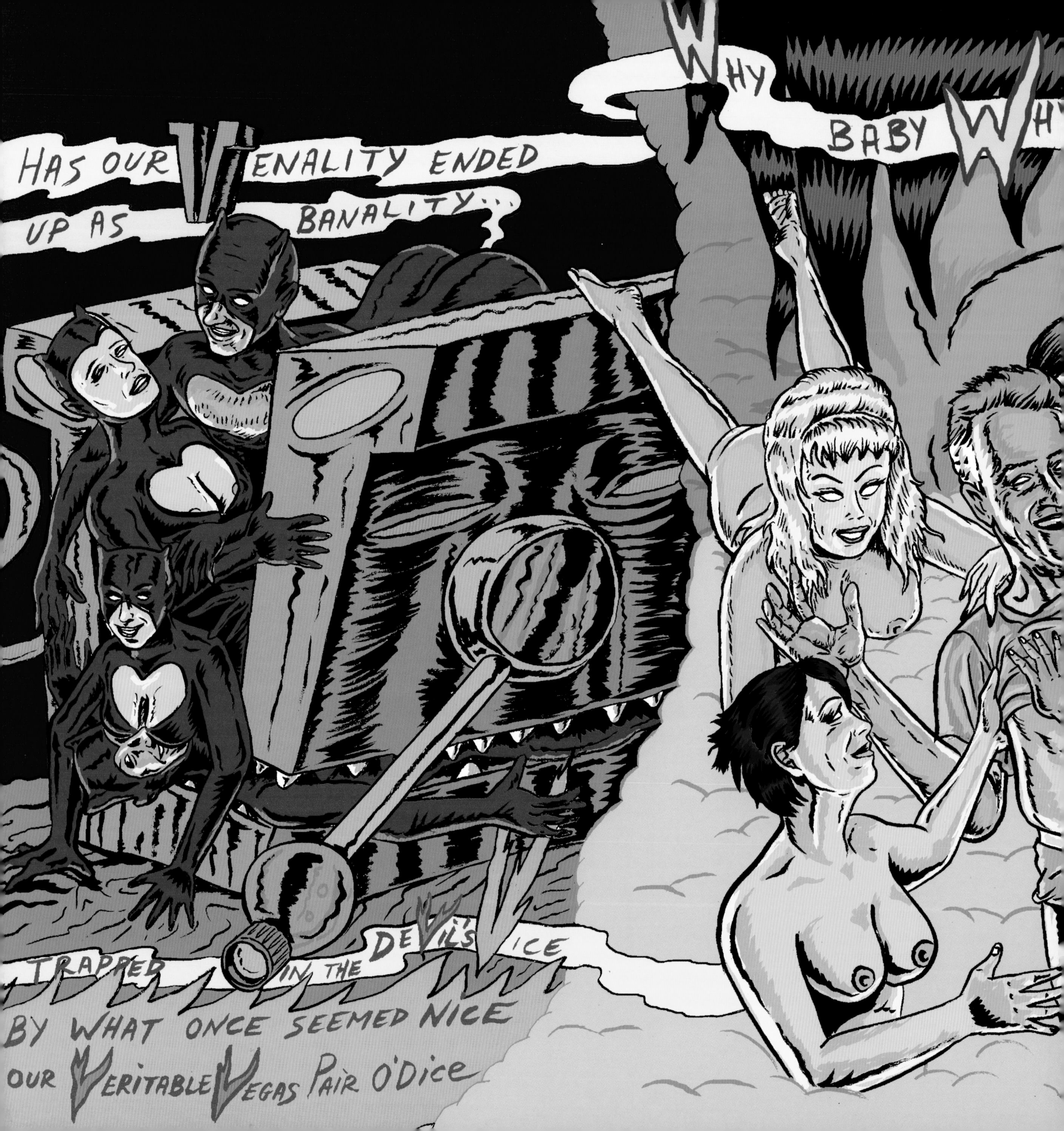

WHY BABY WHY
HAS OUR VENALITY ENDED UP AS BANALITY...
TRAPPED IN THE DEVIL'S VICE
BY WHAT ONCE SEEMED NICE
OUR VERITABLE VEGAS PAIR O'DICE

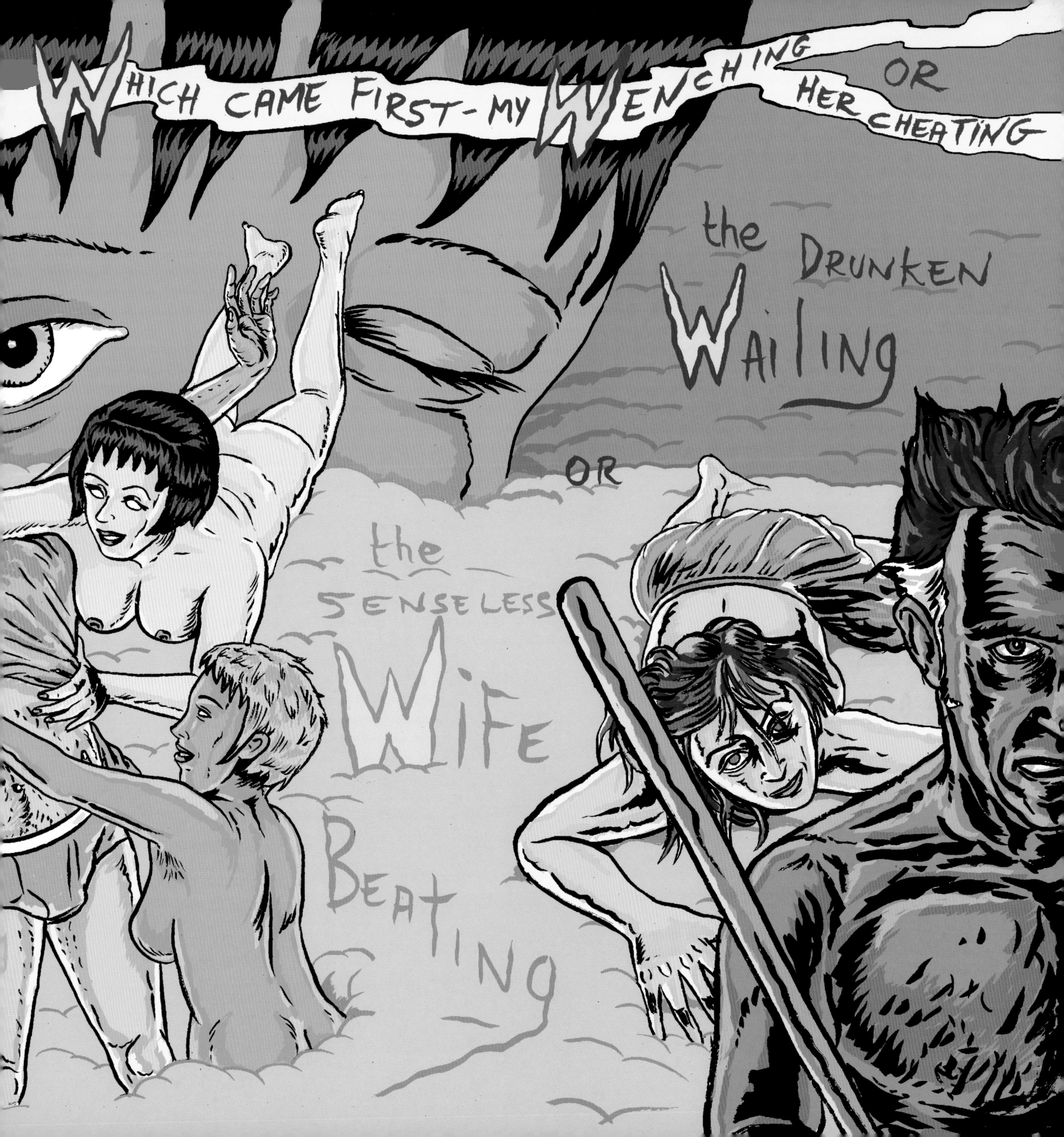

WHICH CAME FIRST - MY WENCHING OR HER CHEATING
the DRUNKEN WAILING
OR
the SENSELESS WIFE BEATING

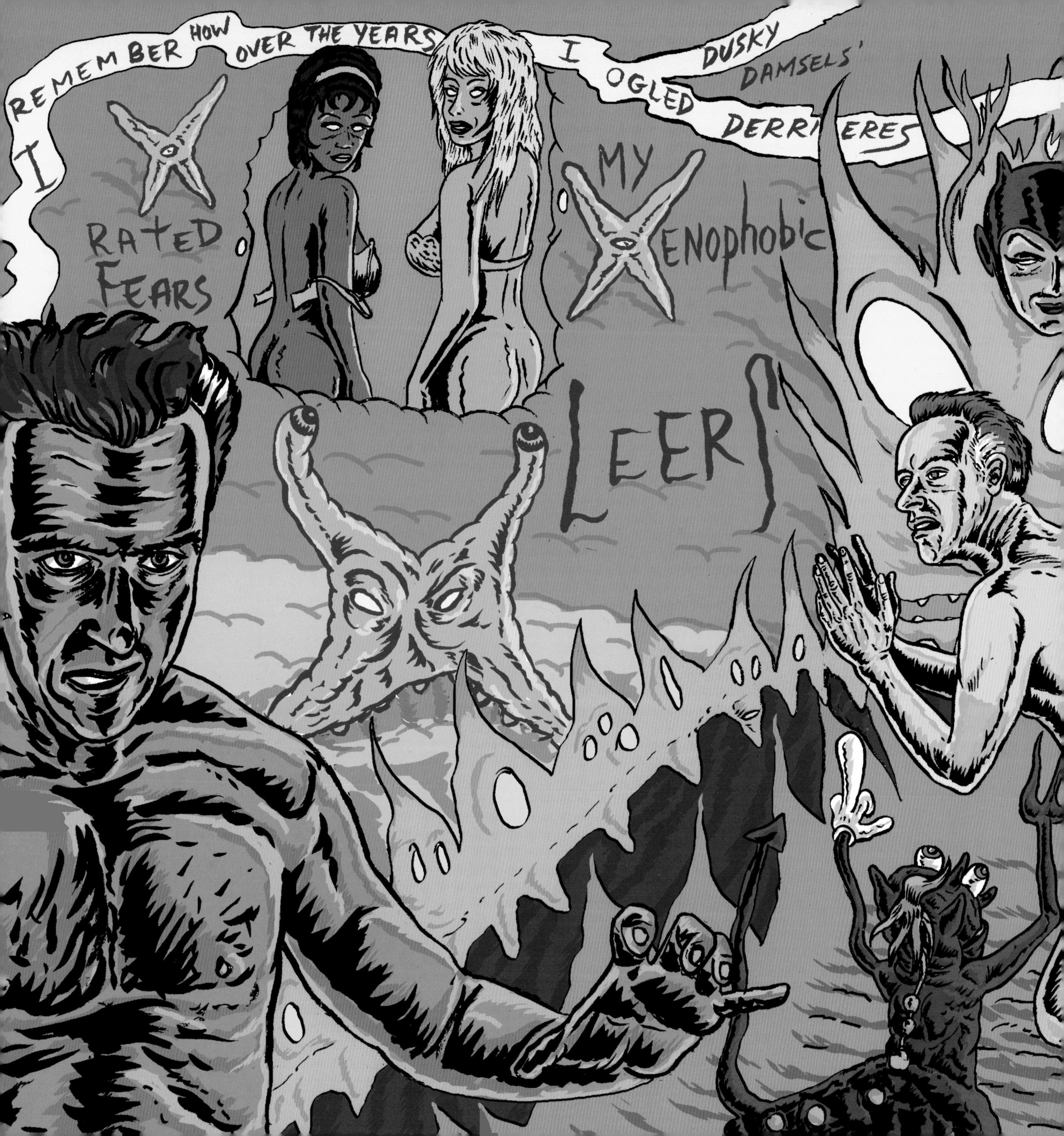
I REMEMBER HOW OVER THE YEARS I OGLED DUSKY DAMSELS' DERRI ERES
RATED FEARS
MY ENOPHOBIC
LEERS

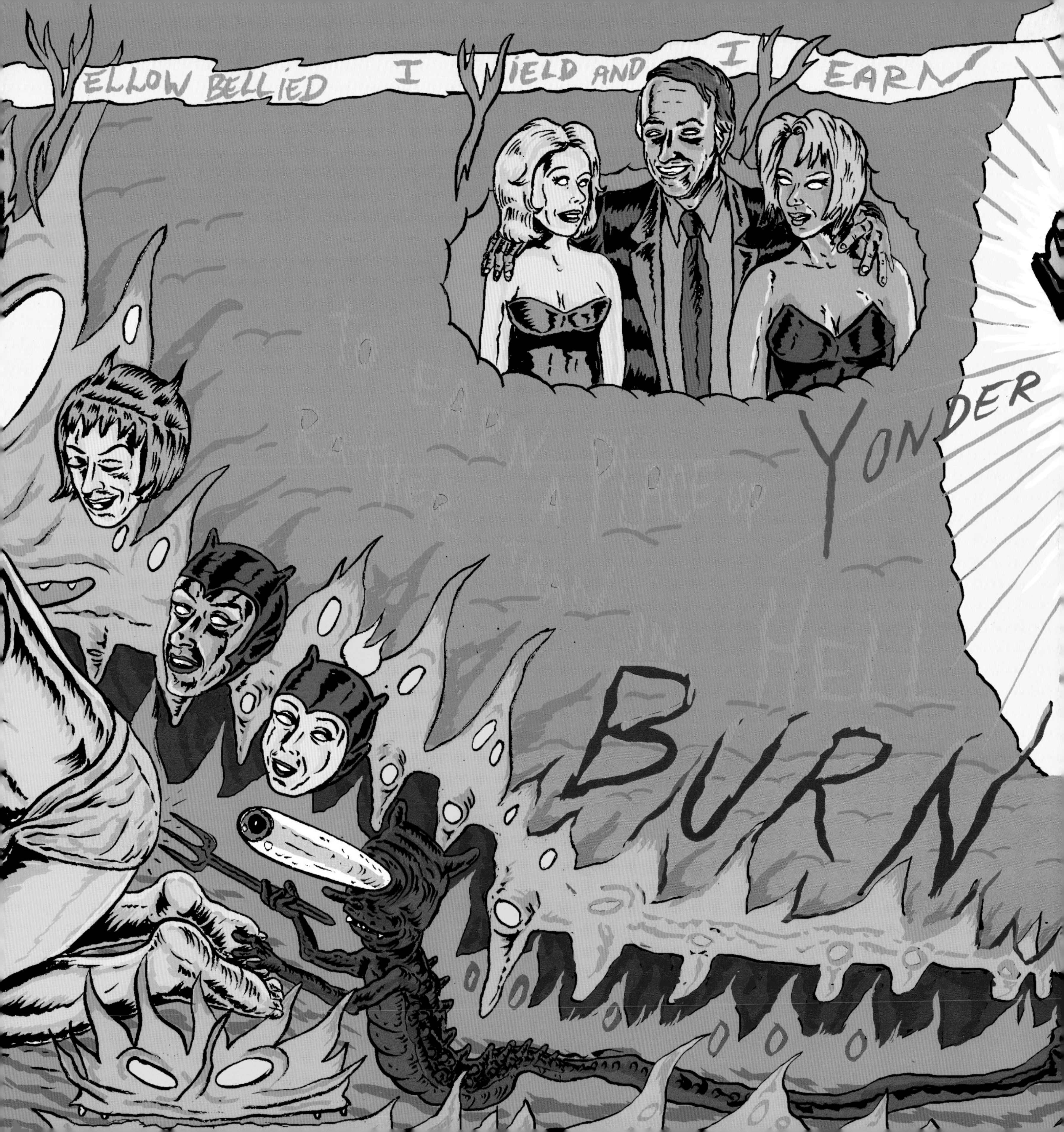
YELLOW BELLIED I YIELD AND I YEARN
YONDER
BURN

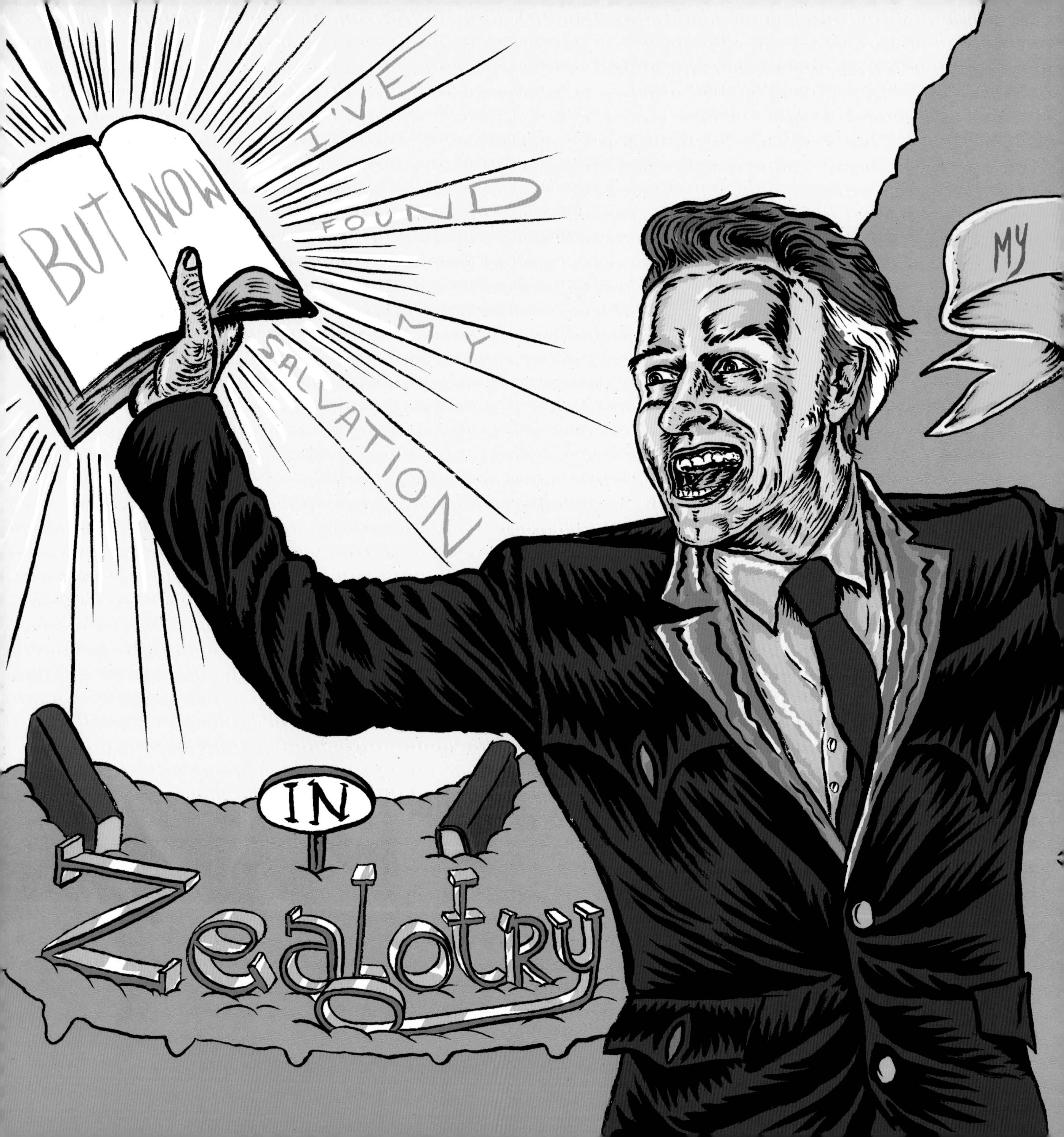

BUT NOW
I'VE FOUND MY SALVATION
IN
ZEALOTRY
MY

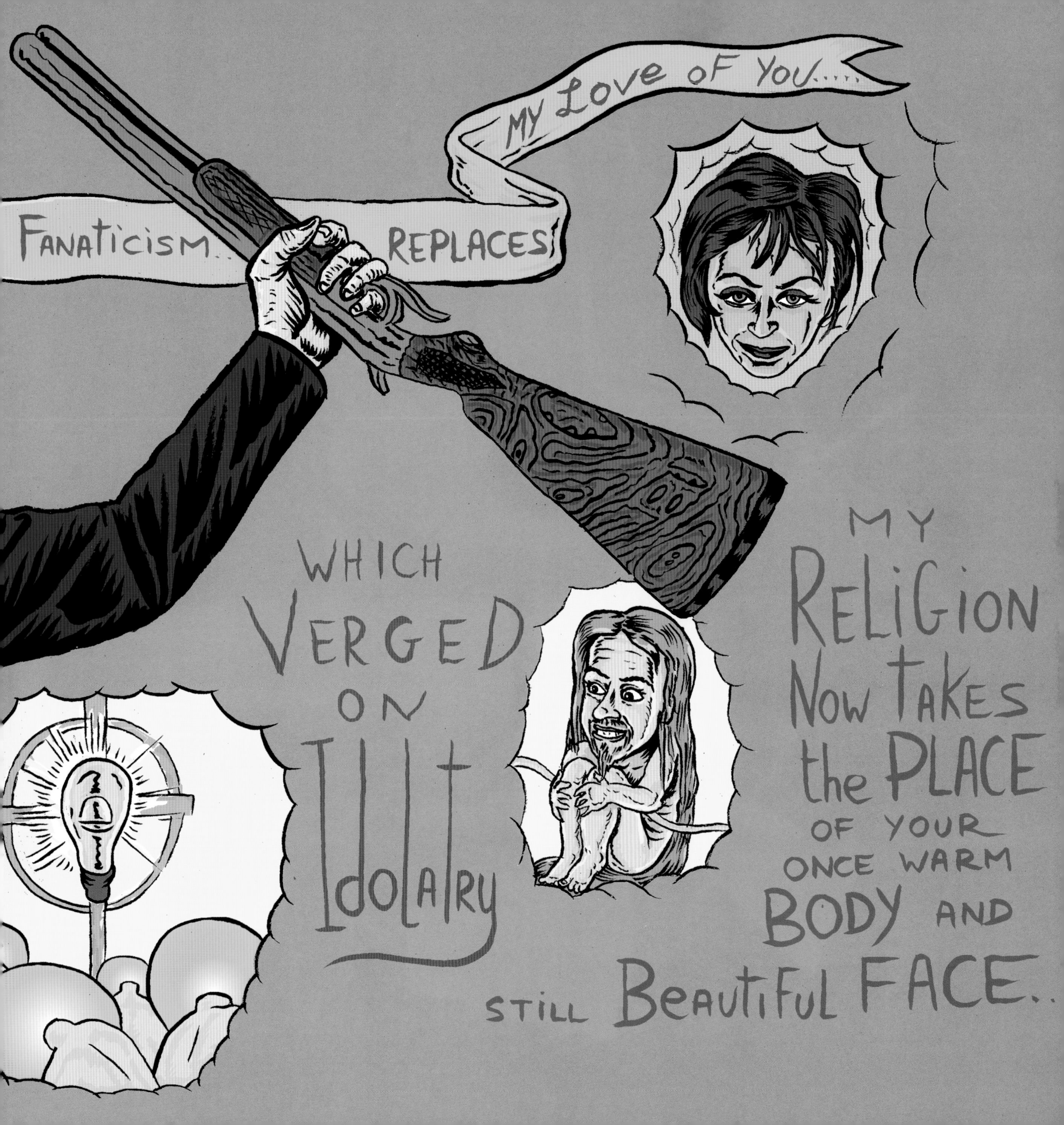
FANATICISM... REPLACES MY LOVE OF YOU.....
WHICH VERGED ON IDOLATRY
MY RELIGION NOW TAKES THE PLACE OF YOUR ONCE WARM BODY AND STILL BEAUTIFUL FACE...

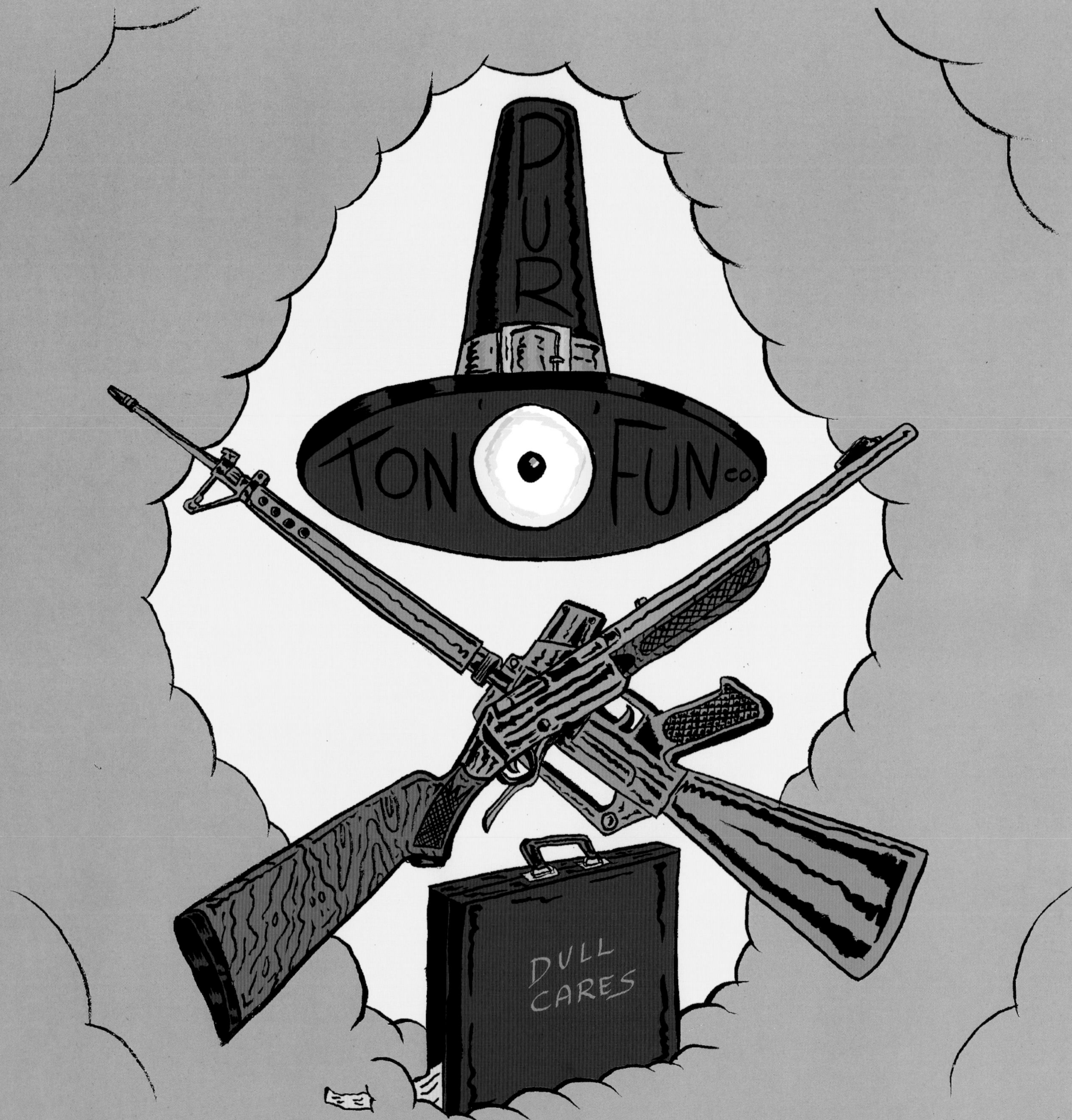
PUR
TON FUN CO.
DULL CARES

Additional titles in the BLAB! Picto-Novelette series include:
Sheep of Fools by Sue Coe and Judith Brody, *Darling Cheri* by Walter Minus,
Struwwelpeter by Bob Staake, *The Magic Bottle* by Camille Rose Garcia, and
Old Jewish Comedians by Drew Friedman.
For more information, please contact: www.fantagraphics.com

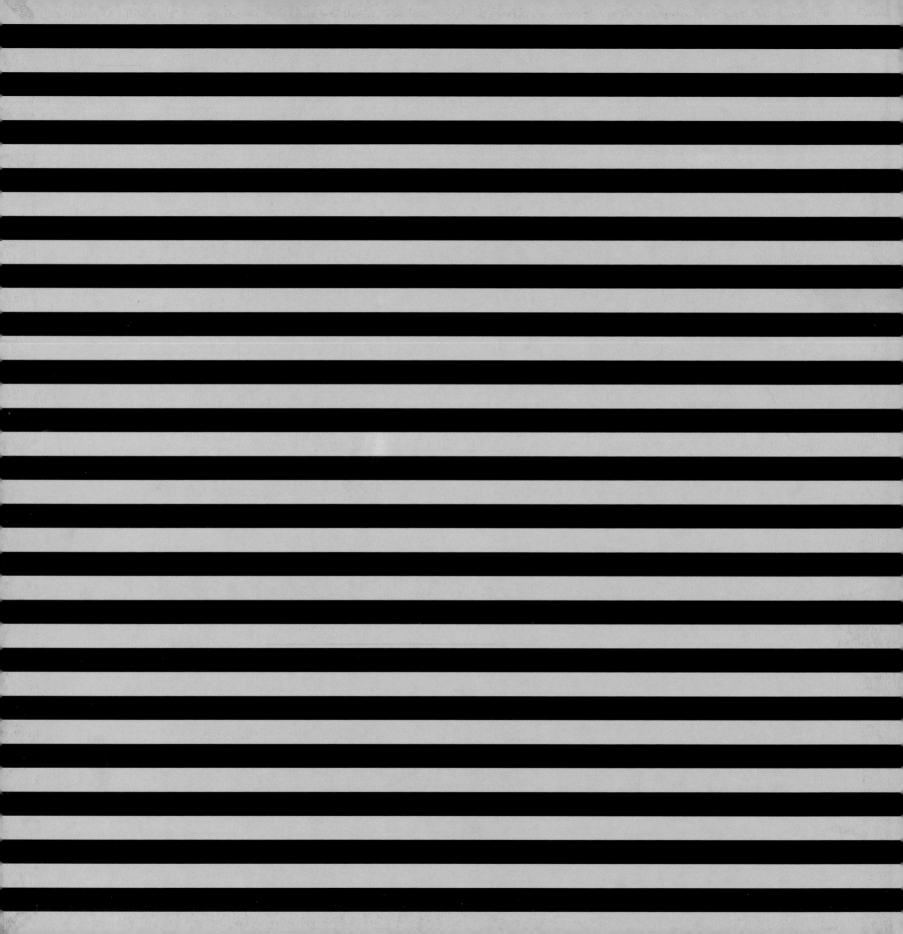